The Broken Circle

To Barb
From Barb!
8/4/19

Barbara Schlichting

The Broken Circle

Formatting by Rik – Wild Seas Formatting

ISBN: 978-1-7324308-6-0

First Lady Press

Other titles by Barb

Single titles

THE BROKEN CIRCLE

First Ladies Mystery Series

Dolley Madison: THE BLOOD SPANGLED BANNER
Mary Lincoln: IF WORDS COULD KILL
Edith Roosevelt: THE CLUE OF THE DANCING BELL

A White House Dollhouse Mystery

Edith Wilson: FOURTEEN POINTS to DEATH

Historical Fiction

BODY ON THE TRACKS

Poetry

WHISPERS FROM THE WIND

Picture Books

Red Shoes by Barbie Marie

Martha Washington: HER FIRST FEW DAYS AS FIRST LADY

Dedication

I dedicate this book to all the missing children. Bless the families and I hope and pray that someday or somehow, you'll meet again.

Special thanks go to my editors Judy Roth and Ramona Long and Rik at Wild Seas Formatting. You all did a great job!

Friends Forever

Friends forever
Friends for life
Friends to skip rope with
Friends to hang out
and watch the boys go by with

Friends to believe in
Friends to find hope with
Friends to grow up
and become adults with

Friends to grow old with
and friends to die with.

Barbara Schlichting

Prologue

It was July of 1969, and Mike Dahl was picking me up. After meticulously ironing my homemade, flowered dress, I raced upstairs to slip it on. With stars in my eyes and butterflies in my stomach I continued dressing for our date. I had about five minutes until his arrival.

When we first met, I had stared into the most beautiful blue eyes in the world and wanted to melt. He stood slightly taller and our knees knocked when we danced. I stepped on his toes, but he smiled and kissed me. I had never felt so beautiful and accepted.

As I clipped my short blonde hair back on the right side, sprayed lilac perfume on my neck, and took another look in the bathroom mirror, the front doorbell rang. I thought my heart would jump out of my chest.

"I'll get it," I called, dashing down the stairs. The bottom stair brought me to the front door, where I opened it. My eyes beheld short, auburn hair, beautiful blue eyes, and the most dazzling smile I'd ever seen. The uniform knocked my socks off!

"Love your dress, my pretty girlfriend. Are you ready?" Mike asked.

"Thank you. I sewed it myself," I said. My warm cheeks gave me away. "I'm ready, my handsome Marine." Mike smiled so brightly, the way he always did when he saw me, but it felt like the first time, every time. "Mom, Dad, I'm leaving."

From the kitchen, I heard advancing footsteps. "You know your curfew," Mom said, walking into the room.

"Yes."

"I'll have her home on time," Mike said.

"I'll hold you to it. Eleven o'clock." Mom looked at us.

"Yes, ma'am."

Mike placed his hand on my lower back and then steered me out the door. When we reached the car, like a gentleman, he opened the door and waited for me to crawl inside before closing it. Once he climbed in and closed his door, he leaned over and kissed me.

"You taste so sweet," he said. He placed his arm around me. "Tonight's a big surprise."

"What are we doing?" I placed my hand on his thigh.

"A drive-in movie, *True Grit*."

"Wow! John Wayne!"

After another longer kiss, he started the car and drove away from the curb. The drive-in was located in the suburbs so it took a few minutes to arrive and park. Together we walked over to the concession stand for popcorn and a shared soda.

Back in the car, our heavy kisses fogged the windows, and Mike rolled his side down. The loudspeaker noise interrupted our embrace.

"We need to be alone," Mike said. He held me in his arms.

"I agree," I said, swatting a mosquito.

"Let's leave," Mike said. "It's time we talked."

"Talked?"

"Yes, about our future," he said and kissed me again.

This kiss was deeper and I barely found my breath. Being with him was like heaven. I snuggled closer and felt warm all over.

With his arm around me, he started the car and slowly we drove the rear lanes until at last reaching the exit. Mike stayed on the roadway until entering the Crosstown Highway 62. Finally, he parked at Minnehaha Falls.

"Why do I feel so sad all of a sudden?" He didn't need to answer. He was leaving tomorrow for Vietnam.

"I think we both know why." He stared into my eyes. "You're the best thing that's ever happened to me."

"I think the same about you. I don't want you to go. We're starting to really get to know each other." Tears filled my eyes.

"I know, sweetheart." Mike held my cheeks in the palms of his hands. "You mean more to me than the sun and the moon." He kissed my lips. "Let me kiss those tears dry, my pretty blondie." He flicked the tears from my cheeks and held a tissue for me to blow my nose.

"Your touch makes me sizzle. My heart wants to burst out of my chest whenever you're near."

"May I?" He slid his palms over my breasts. His

kisses, hot—his breath, heavy.

"This is how we belong. Together," I said, opening my bodice. I returned his kiss, holding him tight within the folds of my arms.

"We are as one and I want it to stay like this forever," Mike said through his kisses. "I want tonight to be memorable." He unzipped my dress and raised the skirt. "Are you sure about this?"

"Yes. I want you." I began unbuttoning his shirt and soon had his pants unzipped.

"I'll remember this moment when I'm far from home." Mike lowered himself and gently entered. "All right?"

"Yes. I want all of you."

Mike kissed me strong and hard, plunging himself farther inside. We devoured each other. When finished, our promise to remain faithful seemed like an eternity of loving each other.

Mike started the engine, and in silence we rode to my house. Inside the house was dark, which allowed us another quiet moment outside the front door.

"I love you, Nancy. You're mine, forever more."

"I love you, Mike. We're made for each other." We kissed. "I'm glad that we did it. I'm glad that you were my first."

"No one is like you. I'm looking forward to my return. Stay as sweet as you are."

"Write soon."

"I will, just as soon as I can."

In the soft moonlight, I watched my handsome man climb into his car and drive away. Tears streamed down my cheeks. I didn't care. It seemed like a very long time before I gathered enough strength to enter the house and go to my room.

Still dressed, I crawled under the covers and cried into my pillow.

Nancy
Chapter One

I slipped from under the warm sheets and tiptoed out to the living room where a full, silver moon greeted me. The light guided me to my plugged-in iPad. Once I sat down and draped a lightweight throw over myself, I reached for it.

I logged into my Facebook account and read old messages, discarding a few. The first unread message was from Sharon. The Dahl family home was for sale. The home where I'd met Mike's family. I'd loved his mom. His dad frightened the life out of me, but in all fairness, I was so shy back then I was scared of my own shadow. We'd grown up in south Minneapolis, Mike in the Longfellow district and I in Hiawatha. Not far from each other.

Yawning, I wrapped the throw tighter as I searched houses for sale in that section of the city. I still lived in the Minneapolis area, Linden, a nearby suburb where I'd taught high school special education classes for thirty years. I'd just retired and lived alone. My husband left me many years ago. His parting words were, "Nancy, there isn't enough room in your heart for two."

It was meant to be this way. Living alone. I didn't mind. Really.

My former life kept me busy, but now it seemed

that memories flooded my mind. Some were sweet and then there were those that weren't. I hated to see Mike's family home sold. After clicking on a few realtor links, I found the house, and it looked the same—still painted white. Purple irises bordered the porch like before, however, the trees were now fully grown. The branches hung down like an umbrella against the glaring sunshine. Staring at the image, I thought of us going up the front steps.

Mike steering me inside the front room and saying, "Mom, I'd like you to meet Nancy." I swear my knees almost buckled from nervousness. My mouth wouldn't move either. Mike's mom sized me up and down, then smiled. "Have a seat." She patted the couch beside her, glanced up at Mike and said, "How about a soda for us?" Mike did just that, then squeezed in right beside me. Our legs touched. I wore a sundress because I knew he was coming, and I would meet his mom. Today, he wore shorts and a t-shirt. His sisters gathered at our feet and giggled. I blushed as I tried to find my voice.

I logged off from the realty site, clicked once again back to my Facebook page, and responded to the message. It was nice of Sharon to tell me about it as well as information about an old classmate, Margo. She wasn't expected to make it through the night. Sharon wrote her cell phone number into the message, and I transferred it to my phone. I said a silent prayer for my lifelong friend. *I should call Judy, but it's too late. Tomorrow.*

Chilled, I crawled under the covers and reached for a tissue to wipe away my tears. Margo was the most loved of us four childhood friends.

Sleep eluded me because thoughts of Margo went around in my mind. She was always fun and happy, smiling all the time. I always felt better around her.

I woke to a ringing phone.

As a retired teacher, every so often I was called to work as a substitute when the demand for teachers was higher than the supply.

It would be a tough day at the middle school because of the assignment—band. I was assured the lesson plans would be easy to follow, that a beginner could handle it. I laughed to myself as I dressed in my suit of armor. Heels, black dress, and red lipstick. I figured that would scare them. I had enough gray hair to make the kids cringe because they'd think of a hated aunt. I wrapped a purple scarf around my neck, slipped into my outerwear, and headed to the kitchen.

The view as I drove the dirt road was of orange and yellow leaves and tinted grasses. I loved the colors of fall. Sweet looking deer stood alongside of the county road, munching their morning meal. After turning onto the main thoroughfare, I traveled near where the Sioux Nation had gathered to control access to the Minnesota river bottoms. Passing the landmark of Fort Snelling, used as an outpost to control the fur trade and further uprising from the Native People, it wasn't long before I turned onto the school lot and parked.

The secretary smiled, handed over the substitute file folder, told me what room, and I was off toward it. Although I was early, there were children already outside the door waiting to drop off instruments.

"You the sub?" a student asked. She wore pants so tight I cringed when she bent over to retrieve her saxophone case.

"Yep. Aren't you lucky?" I grinned, hoping it'd make both of us feel better.

"Whatever," another student replied. I thought her makeup of speckled eyes was a bit too much, but who was I to say?

So much for breaking the ice.

I stepped inside and the waiting students followed with one flipping the lights on.

"Thanks," I said. I picked up the laid out lesson plans as the kids stored their instruments. They left the room, to return during different periods. The lesson plan read: *If you're not a music teacher, show a movie. It's best that way. They're in the back cabinet. If you don't know how to run the machine, someone will show you what to do.*

"Good," I murmured.

I went to the cabinet and chose *The Music Man* because it seemed appropriate for the class.

During break time, I found Judy's number and called.

"I'm sorry, Nancy, but I have a class coming in. Call me tonight."

"Will do." *Was her speech slurred or was I imagining it?*

I drove home with the radio turned off, my thoughts on Margo and Judy.

The TV remained on mute until the evening news. While a bowl of chicken soup warmed in the microwave, I checked into Facebook. In the message column, one appeared. It was also addressed to Judy.

Hi, my mother, Margo, spoke highly of her friends. Sadly, she passed away late last night. The funeral is Saturday, 10 o'clock at Bethany Lutheran and Sharon is officiating. I hope that you can make it. Sorry for the late notification, but I've been really busy with arrangements. Mary.

Tears filled my eyes. Somehow, I managed a short note with condolences. I knew I'd go to the funeral. We'd done everything together when we were kids. How could I possibly let my best friend go to the hereafter without me being near? *How can I grow old without her?*

As I went to the kitchen, I said a silent prayer for Margo and Mary. I hoped Mary wouldn't take it too hard. The tissue box was nearby so I reached for one to wipe my eyes. "I can't believe she's gone and I'll never see her again," I sobbed and eventually dried my eyes and blew my nose.

After I'd pulled myself together, I gave Sharon a call. She answered immediately.

"I knew you'd call," she said. I could almost see her swish back her long brown hair. "You're coming?"

"Of course. I contacted Judy earlier today, but she was busy. I'll call after I eat." I waited a beat before continuing, "This has to be hard on you?"

"I didn't know her as well as you did, but, yes, it is," Sharon said.

I debated asking about the house, if it had sold.

"How are you?"

"I'm fine. I get lonesome, but doing all right."

"I have a great idea, why not stay here Saturday night? We'll have Judy stay, too. We can talk about old times."

"It won't be too much for you? Why don't you come here? I've room for you and Judy."

"No, I'd like you both here. I'll have so much food left from the funeral and I bet there'll be phone calls later in the afternoon about the funeral service and things like Mary's address for sympathy cards. Also, I have the morning's sermon."

"I didn't think of that."

"We'll eat whatever is left from the funeral that Mary doesn't want."

"Sounds good. I'll contact Judy. Thanks, Sharon."

"It'll be great to see you two again. It's the same address. See you tomorrow."

The chicken soup was already a week old but still delicious. After cleaning up the kitchen, I went to pack. As I neatly folded my overnight clothes and tossed in an outfit for Sunday, I thought of Margo and all the fun we used to have.

After school, her mom set out home-baked chocolate chip cookies and chocolate milk as a treat for us. Her dad never seemed to be home, but he worked long hours at Minneapolis Moline building tractors. My dad had worked on Hiawatha Avenue at the Grain Elevator. Sharon's and Mike's dad worked as a mechanic. Those were trusted times, innocent times.

I removed my smartphone from my pocket, pressed the correct button for Judy, and waited for an answer. I left a voice message: *The funeral's at 10:00 at*

Bethany. Sharon's officiating and asked for us to spend the night at her place. Bring your old pictures, and we'll pick out a few and put together something for Mary. I'll have my computer with me. Don't bring any food as she'll have plenty. See you soon. Nancy. After disconnecting, I said, "I wish she'd answered."

I took an early shower and reached for my old school albums and brought them into the living room. Once I'd settled in with a cup of tea and the TV turned to my favorite station, *Hallmark,* I opened the first photo album.

The first few pages were of me as a child with my two brothers, Tommy and Peter. Tommy and I used to pedal our bikes to the little beach of Lake Nokomis. Peter was a few years younger than us big kids. Sometimes, if we were good, Mom gave us money to stop for an ice cream cone. Life was so much simpler back in the fifties and early sixties. As I studied the photos, I realized just how much time had really changed and how innocent we kids were back in that era.

The next few pages showed photos of me with friends, and that was when I came upon glimpses of the past with my girlfriends. Birthday parties, overnight sleep-ins, boys and girls parties. Spin-the-bottle and hopefully not kiss a fool or someone with a face full of acne.

There, in the center of the larger photo, was Margo. She was all dressed up for the last day of sixth grade. Beside her stood me, Judy, and Vicky. I wondered whatever happened to Vicky? My heart went out to her mom and brother. I removed the photo and set it aside to start a pile of photos for a flash drive to later gift to Mary. Several photos of us girls were removed and placed in the pile. Some of them were of lying in the sun, slumber parties, or backyard swimming pools. The best one was of bobbing for apples and Margo dripping wet with an apple stuck in her mouth. I chuckled. That had been a fun party at her house. I couldn't wait to see the girls' faces light up when they saw this particular photo. High school photos of chorus and dances came later, and then Sharon was in the photos. We'd become close friends when I began dating her brother. Once Mike went to Vietnam, he asked for my hand in marriage, which I accepted. Upon his return, he broke the engagement, and I never understood why. Sharon would always be my good friend, but because of the breakup, things have never been the same between us. When I heard about Mike's marriage, it became even harder to be her friend. It hurt too much.

I was completely lost in my thoughts.

Sharon always helped to stamp out fires between us girls, especially when it came to our attire and who took what outfit from one of our closets. We also stripped ourselves down and grabbed each other's clothes. That was Margo's idea. We did that at dances to throw the boys off. Of course, I was the tallest and skinniest so few could fit into my dresses, especially Margo because she was so short. Judy was the bravest. She'd strut around like a little tart sometimes, and we'd laugh. Afterward, she'd tuck herself back up again. She only did that when we were alone, though, the tart bit. We were all too shy. I was too thin. Sharon was so thoughtful and kind. She fit in with us like a true friend.

Mike was seventeen and I was sixteen. It was, the summer before my senior year. Because Sharon grew up in a different neighborhood from me she went to another school. She would've been my sister-in-law.

My thoughts went to Judy and Sharon. *Are they happy?*

It'd been years since we'd all been together—1970 prom night before Vicky's abduction. I really miss her friendship. Her wit. Her—period. Margo worked as a secretary at a school in Minneapolis until too ill to continue. We'd stayed in contact, but just barely. I could kick myself for not seeing her more often. She'd had the one daughter, Mary.

I began to wonder silly things such as who had the most gray hair? Judy had moved to Madison, Wisconsin, right after high school, and barely kept in contact. I tried to think of the number of years it'd been since we'd met but couldn't remember. She'd always been interested in studying German. Did she have her doctorate now?

Would the three of us recognize each other? Sharon, of course, would still remind me of Mike with her beautiful blue eyes and long hair like her mother's. Margo became involved with her own life, as did Judy and I.

My excitement grew to see both Judy and Sharon and spend time poring through all the photos and talking about old times.

The howling wind refocused my thoughts and I looked outside, only to shiver. Freezing rain speckled the front living room window. I worried about Judy because of her earlier slurred speech and long drive.

Graduation had been in June of 1970. It was about the time Mike was due for his month's leave from his yearlong tour of duty. I'd accepted his marriage proposal and hoped for a ring upon his return. His volume of letters had slowed, and I'd begun to worry about him. Was he safe? Was he injured? Didn't he love me anymore?

I knew I was in dangerous waters so I tried to shove all thoughts of him from my mind.

He told me to forget about him. What happened in 1970 that split us up?

I wondered what the weekend would bring, a renewal or not?

What sort of shadow lay hidden about Mike I was yet to discover? Whenever I'd dare ask about him, Sharon would change the subject. What happened to Mike that would make her avoid speaking of her favorite brother?

Judy
Chapter Two

Packing was the last thing on my mind as I threw my nightgown into the suitcase. I wondered what to wear to the funeral? What was fashionable nowadays? I hadn't attended one in ages, mostly because I didn't believe in them. But, it was for Margo. She was the dearest person who ever walked the earth. My parents always had fists raised or beer bottles flying through the air at each other. Margo always stayed with me, and no one else was brave enough to handle the commotion and anger in my house.

Was there a hereafter?

I was having trouble believing that Margo died. I knew I'd miss her something fierce, but doggone it! It had been years since last we'd met. Why did her funeral have to bring the bunch of us together? Why couldn't it be a happier occasion, such as Nancy finally getting some closure with her soldier boy? Why hadn't Sharon ministered in Africa?

What were their thoughts about me? Poor Judy? Well, that was none of their business, and I planned to keep it that way. I taught college level German and loved it. I had my doctorate in German. What did it matter who we were?

The four of us started school together. Me, Nancy, Margo and Vicky. Kindergarten. Boy, was that a long time ago, and Sharon joined us in our senior year. Margo, with her freckles and curly red hair, lit up the room. Oh, but she was grand. Always full of energy and smiles. Her presence alone made you smile. She liked pulling pranks, too. I remember the day she brought in a can of sardines for snack time. The stink! Yikes! The remembrance of the laughter from the class, plus nose pinching, made me suddenly chuckle.

I absolutely loved Margo. She was the happiest and best out of the four of us.

Vicky was smarter than a bug. She could get A's in science and math like nobody's business. I barely scratched the surface and passed by the skin of my teeth. *Will she ever be found?*

I reached for my ready-made drink of whiskey and soda. A good stiff drink before driving would calm my nerves.

Did it really have to be Margo to go first? *She wouldn't have left me alone that night had she known. Are the other girls keeping secrets?* I wonder.

With my empty drink glass in hand, I went into the hallway, pulling my suitcase behind me. My husband had divorced me fifteen years ago because of my drinking. The bottle didn't have a bottom. He never remarried and we see each other on a regular basis.

The ringing phone interrupted my thoughts, and I answered once I saw the caller's identity.

"Judy? Judy Hokstad?"

"Nancy? Is it really you?" I asked.

"Yes. Please stay at Sharon's after the funeral."

"I will. I'm going straight to a motel right now. I've

made reservations." My fingers shook as I lit my smoke. "This is a toughie. I almost wish it'd been me."

"Don't ever say that. We're still the best of friends—all four of us. We will be forever!" Nancy said, but I knew what she was thinking.

Why Margo?

"You're right. All for one and one for all," I tried to say in a cheery voice. I hesitated a moment before continuing, "The wind is bad and it might be misting a little bit." I took another drag from my cigarette, watching the smoke curl around the empty glass.

"Safe travels."

"Thanks. I'll see you tomorrow at church."

I placed the phone on the cradle and sobbed. Blowing my nose, I began to wonder if it was possible to drive to Minneapolis? It was at least a seven-hour drive and the hour was getting late. I took a deep breath. Then another before I felt energized. I threw a full whiskey flask into the suitcase, took my purse, keys, and walked out the door, shutting it behind me.

Did she have to call now? Right when I was leaving?

The gas tank was full when I backed from the garage and pressed the button to close the overhead door. The interstate entrance wasn't far, fortunately. I figured that I'd be tucked into my motel bed about 12:30. I wouldn't fall asleep while driving because of the pill I'd taken before leaving and the "one for the road" drink.

The drive won't seem so long, knowing a flask was also tucked inside my purse. There was a wayside rest road sign near the Minnesota border, but it had a closed sign over it. I continued until a fast food restaurant appeared. I signaled and exited, driving toward the drive-thru.

After using the facilities, I ordered a burger and small beverage. Once in the car, it seemed fitting to add a touch from the flask into the soda. It wasn't strong enough for my taste, so I added a bit more. In a few minutes, I was back on the interstate and heading toward Stillwater. Time was on my side, at only eleven o'clock. It occurred to me that we should meet ahead of time and try to sit together. It seemed like a great idea. I quickly finished the remnants of my burger and drank down the soda.

Should I send a message?

I sped along beside a fast moving semi-trailer, then removed the flask from my purse and took a swallow of whiskey. A deer shot out from the roadside woods. I swerved, barely missing it. Shaken, I stopped by the side of the road to catch my breath. *Time to calm my nerves.* I took another sip. It took a few minutes to catch my wits, and then I picked up my phone. I was able to locate the needed numbers easily, touched the right buttons, and sent both a message. It read: *what time meet church?* Now, I just needed a reply. Afterward I drove onto the road when it cleared of traffic.

I turned up the radio and let my thoughts go to the four of us and how much fun we used to have at slumber parties, school dances, and car racing up and down Lake Street. Picking up guys at the dances, or should I say getting picked up! Then our senior year and meeting older guys—from the U of M—and how we'd thought we were so grown up attending those sorority parties. Thank heavens our parents didn't learn about it. Not that mine would have cared.

A semi-truck barreled up behind me, honking, and then another. I glanced at my speedometer and realized I wasn't going fast enough—50—so I sped up slightly. A light mist started falling, and I turned on the windshield wipers. My rearview mirror showed both lanes populated with semi-trucks and cars. My phone chirruped, and I reached for it.

The message from Sharon read: *9:30 church.* A steady stream of cars zipped past, causing me to shudder from the speed.

Vehicles whizzed past me right and left, it didn't matter which lane I drove on. I gripped the steering wheel for dear life as I stared out the windshield. Wasn't there a shortcut? If my memory served correctly, the next two-lane highway would bring me to Silver Lake Road so I decided to exit. Soon I was alone on the poorly lit, winding road. *This road is worse.* I stopped beside the nearest fast food restaurant to use the facilities.

Nancy hadn't responded, so I sent another message to her. Back on the highway, I realized it wouldn't take long before I'd be at my destination. Clouds blocked the moon, and the black sky was oppressive. The lamps lighting the two-lane highway seemed foggy and dim. I glanced at my phone when it sounded and read: *where are you.* I frowned because I wanted more from Nancy. Not just from Nancy, but from both of them.

Visibility worsened. Snow began falling, unusual for mid-October. The road became slick, so I slowed down to accommodate the weather conditions.

I answered my ringing phone and said, "Hello!"

"Nancy, here, checking in. Where are you?"

"Getting closer, not sure where. I took a back road."

"Are you lost?" Nancy said.

"I hope not," I said, wondering if it was possible. "Maybe I should stop for directions?"

"What highway are you on?"

"Last I saw a sign, it was 95."

"That doesn't sound right, shouldn't you be on 94?" Nancy said. "Here I am, telling you where to go."

"Honey, I'm used to people telling me where to go and how to do it," I said. "Don't worry, Miss Minnesota Nice, I'll figure it out," I said. I hoped she didn't notice the slurring.

"You sound funny. Are you okay?"

"Yes," I said. "I'll drive slow." I hiccupped. I'll bet she heard that. "Sorry, I coughed."

"See you in the morning," Nancy said, disconnecting.

Truthfully, I didn't know where on earth I was. The visibility was abysmal, the road signs few and far between. I was lost and knew it. I pulled over to the shoulder and let a few cars go by as I tried to focus and get my sense of directions in place. The snow made it impossible to see. The GPS on my phone showed I was headed in the right direction. I widened the view on

; phone and deciphered I wasn't too far off the mark. If I kept going on this road, it would take me to Interstate 94, which was what I should've stayed on instead of exiting from. I sent Nancy a message: *I'm going in the right direction and will be on 94 asap.* I sent it, turned my signal on, and merged with traffic.

A large truck passed me, which made my little car shimmy. The wipers couldn't keep up with the snow, so I cranked up the defroster blower and heat. Oncoming traffic headlights were dimmed from the snow. An oncoming passing car scared me, and I swerved to miss it. My fists clenched the steering wheel, and my eyes were wide open. My heart pounded. Another fool tried passing, racing around the other car. I held my breath. *Is this how it'll end?*

Was that a mailbox by the side of the road, or a deer? I blinked twice, to make sure it hadn't moved. No bright luminescent eyes staring at me. Yes, it was a mailbox. I was safe. It wouldn't walk out in front of me.

It seemed colder in the car, and I adjusted the heater. Why was the window so foggy? I grabbed a glove and wiped the inside windshield, only to find a thick, gray film remaining. *Is the defroster going out on me? Did the heater dysfunction, again? Sure, it must be the gasses from the defroster and heater fogging the inside windshield, turning it gray, as it happened once before.*

As I drove, I rubbed off more of the slime from the inside window. I realized that something was definitely, seriously dysfunctional on the car. I glanced at my clock and found it after midnight. My only hope was to keep wiping the film from the front. First thing in the morning, I'd be contacting my auto club.

An icy patch brought me to a skidded halt beside the side of the road. I reached for my flask and sucked out a drop before sealing it and placing it inside of the glove compartment. A few cars drove around me, with one honking. I took the time to scrape off the thick film from the windows, only to see it cloud up instantly. I got the scraper from under the seat, leaned forward, and began slowly driving while scraping. Cars honked and kept passing. I knew I should stay on the shoulder, but I didn't want to take the time.

Slush flew up and caught me off guard. Cars raced passed as I entered the interstate. Twenty miles left. Traffic was light. Another patch of ice caught me and I skidded.

Fear raced up and down my spine. The headlights of an oncoming car looked me in the eye.

I blinked.

I swerved and landed in the ditch.

Nancy
Chapter Three

I often wondered why Sharon hadn't ministered in Africa? Now she's settled and ministers at my church. I shouldn't call it, "my church" because I attend, whenever the moment hits, a church closer to home. Ever since my husband, Paul, left, I've turned into a recluse. It's rare that I go out especially at night. I do have a few girlfriends that I go to a movie with or join for coffee, but being alone is how I like it. I try to convince myself that I'm the happiest alone, but holidays, I miss Paul and wish for him the best in life, more than what I could offer him.

I hadn't gotten over my first love at the time of our marriage and probably never would. Mike was fun, kind and full of energy while Paul was the opposite. Paul kept to himself and rarely shared his inner soul to me. Things may have been different if he had.

I absolutely loved Margo. She was the happiest and best out of us. Sharon came along and fit in nicely with the four of us.

My excitement grew to see both Judy and Sharon and spend time poring through all the photos, talking about old times. My only wishes would be that Vicky was with us and for Margo to still be alive.

Freezing rain speckled the front living room window. I worried about Judy because of her earlier slurred speech and long drive.

I hoped she wouldn't drink and drive. Was her slurred speech caused from too much alcohol already?

The photos had really jogged my memory. I sat back down and paged through the remaining albums while keeping an eye on the weather station.

Another photo of us playing dolls, one of hopscotch and another riding our bikes. We lived in such close proximity to each other that we were always together. Smiling, I thought about playing dress-up with Margo's mom's high-heeled shoes. Vicky's family room and pretending that we played guitars like the Beatles. Judy always played Ringo's part on the drums. We'd style our hair like them. It's funny to think about these things.

But, did it really have to be Margo who went first? Or Vicky never found?

It was at least a seven-hour drive and the hour was getting late. I figured Judy would be tucked into her motel bed about 12:30. She would have to stop to eat or get gas for the car, which added at least a half-hour to the drive. She may not send the message until 1 o'clock.

I switched the TV station to the local network, setting the photos and albums aside. The news reports weren't very promising for a decent drive between Wisconsin and the Twin Cities. Freezing rain was covering the interstate systems, and there wasn't a chance for a let up in rain for several hours. The driving was at a slower pace than normal with visibility down to a few feet.

"Judy, pull over," I whispered. The last thing in the world that I wanted was for her to land in a ditch or hospital because of the driving conditions. I also didn't want to bury another good, long time friend.

In my desk drawer, I found a new memory stick and put it into my computer's flash drive. As I scanned and added the photos onto it, I tried to keep my thoughts happy. Judy needed all the positive energy I could muster to bring her safely to the motel. I thought of happy thoughts. Going to the zoo and playing on the playground in school. Choir and singing Christmas songs. Reading Betsy, Tacy and Tib books and Nancy Drew, then sharing them. When finished, I grabbed the book I was reading and laid back in my recliner to read, keeping the TV on. I figured the television light would keep me awake.

At midnight, my phone dinged. Judy had sent a message. It read: *Just crossed the border.*

I responded: *Good. Be careful.*

I turned back to the weather station and let my thoughts go to our senior year and meeting older guys—from the U of M—and how we'd thought we were so grown up being invited to those sorority parties. I never attended. I was engaged to Mike at the time so I never attended any of them.

Nervous energy overtook me and I went to my china cabinet and removed the glassware. When the sink was full of hot sudsy water, I got busy washing the glasses. When I'd dried and replaced them inside the cabinet, I went back out to the living room.

Visuals from the local station broadcast showed

a steady stream of cars and vehicles in the ditches. Clouds blocked the moon, and the black sky looked oppressive. The lamps lighting the two-lane highway seemed foggy and dim. Visibility worsened. Snow began falling, which meant the roads were slicker.

I wanted to send Judy a message to see where she was but didn't think it would be wise to disrupt her driving.

Judy sent a message: *I will be on 94 asap.*

I responded. Okay

Now I had an idea as to where she was and could better time her arrival at the motel. I kept my eyes peeled on the traffic situation. Slush flew up from the motorists. Cars raced past each other as if they were play toys. I glanced at the wall clock. Judy should be soon exiting onto the service road. Not much time left and she'll be safe, I told myself. I hadn't wanted to go to bed yet, I needed to know she was safe. I placed a pillow on an arm of the couch and tucked a throw over myself to wait it out. I was sure she'd send me a message once she'd dropped her suitcase inside the room and turned on the lights. The TV was still on so I found an old favorite movie to watch. My hope was that it would prevent me from falling asleep.

I opened my eyes to sunlight peeking through the shadows from the trees.

Sleeping the night on the couch caused me to groan and my bones to creek as I flipped back the throw from myself and tried to sit. My legs felt stiff and sore. My back muscles as tight as a rope. Slowly I eased myself up to stand and glanced at the cuckoo clock. It was seven. I reached for my phone to check messages. There weren't any. I wondered if it was too early to call Judy?

I turned the station to the local news just as a reporter showed a horrible car crash on the interstate. The reporter said that it happened about one o'clock. In my heart, I knew it was Judy and she had to be in a hospital. This time I didn't hesitate, I called Sharon.

"Sharon, have you seen the news?"

"What time is it? What's up?"

"Turn on the news," I said. I stared at the screen. "It's important. I think our Judy is in the hospital."

"I'm sure she's fine." I could almost picture Sharon swishing her long hair from her shoulders. "I've got it on now."

"I have a bad feeling about this. Really bad," I said. My heart seemed to pound in my ears. "She'd been drinking. I'm almost positive."

"We'll hear from Judy soon," Sharon said gently. "She had farther to go."

"I hope you're right," I said.

"Let's say a prayer for her," Sharon suggested and I clasped my hands. "Dear Lord, please look after all the accident victims. Amen."

"Amen."

"All we can do now is put it in God's hands," Sharon said. "Better?"

"Yes."

"Hopefully we'll hear soon," Sharon said. "Send me messages when you receive information. I should be at the church by eight as there are plenty for me to look after. I'll look for you about 9:30, then we can view Margo together."

"It'll give us a few extra minutes with Margo and to explore the church—you know—see how it's changed over the years."

"See you soon."

We disconnected. I went to stand in front of the window and stared across the street at the icy windshields from my neighbor's cars. While I spent a moment thinking about the day ahead, I retrieved the remote control and switched to another local station. The report caused me to drop onto the couch.

All my questions were answered right on the big screen. *A roll over. The driver spun out of control and was taken by ambulance to a local hospital. The name wasn't being disclosed because of reaching the next of kin. The ice and snow played a major factor in the accident, but the driver was under the influence of alcohol with an empty bottle inside the vehicle. Since the driver wore a seatbelt, she will survive.* The video of the crash site was frightening.

This time, I was certain it was her. I reached for a tissue and cried. "Not Judy. This can't happen again. Not before I see her. We need time. The three of us need a chance to renew our spirits and talk about old times." I grabbed a few extra tissues.

It took several minutes until finally I gathered my thoughts. First I called the hospitals to locate her and left my name as a local contact. I discovered Judy was admitted into Hennepin County Medical Center, which was right in downtown Minneapolis. It didn't take too long before a head nurse reached me. She was listed as stable. Visiting hours weren't until much later, of course, and I didn't want to wake her with a phone call. Sharon needed to hear the news so I sent a text message, reassuring her that Judy was doing okay, and I'd keep her informed.

The day would be tough enough with Margo's funeral, and now Judy in the hospital only added to the misery. The automatic coffee maker started sputtering and groaning, reminding me I still had things to do. With a full cup of coffee in hand, I went upstairs to finish packing and make sure the house was in order in case Judy should need to convalesce. She'd be welcome to stay here for a few a days unless, of course, the university or her attorney requested her immediate return.

It was minutes later when the phone rang.

"Hello," I said, answering it.

"Sharon here. Just checking in." I heard the anguish in her voice. "How are you?"

"Managing," I said. "I plan to go to the hospital before the service."

"We can go together afterward, too," Sharon said.

"You'll have plenty to take care of. Don't worry. I'll duck out after the luncheon and fetch her," I said. I knew I needed to change the subject.

"I've turned the news on," Sharon said. "I see she was drinking by the news report."

"Unfortunately, it's true," I said. My thoughts went to Mike and the life we never had instead of staying on Judy, but Sharon kept me focused. "Make sure Mary saves me a place right beside her since I'll be late."

"I will," Sharon said. "I'm so cold, it's like I'm numb."

"That's because it's so traumatic. We'll have to really hug each other tight, tonight," I said. "Time for me to dress if I plan to make it to the funeral on time. You'll be wonderful."

"Thanks."

We disconnected and I let out a long breath, then glanced at my shaking hand. It was the first time in years I wished I smoked because I could sure use a cigarette right about now. Sharon's proposal of us three together sounded good. Maybe it was the right way for us to get reacquainted. I felt so out of sorts.

I dressed in a pair of dress black pants, a white blouse, and a maroon sweater. I had matching earrings and necklace, so I put them on. I had planned to dress up, but going in and out between the hospital, church, cemetery, and then the church luncheon, the temperature would be too cold to wear a dress. Another stiff cup of coffee was in order to keep me moving.

It took me a while before my wits were gathered and I felt better. I looked in the mirror and saw a young, blonde, brown-eyed girl, seventeen, blotchy from another hard cry after her soldier boy kissed her and said tomorrow he was leaving for Nam and could he write? I slumped onto the bed and blew my nose for the umpteenth time.

I went for a Tylenol and water, hoping it would

help me focus. Push my emotions aside. I took several deep breaths, blew my nose and wiped my eyes and shifted my gaze to the suitcase. *Buck up, Nancy, where's your courage?*

Once downstairs with the suitcase and albums, I decided a cup of strong coffee from a nearby drive-thru was in order.

With my remote control, I turned the engine over so by the time I'd placed the suitcase in the trunk and crawled in behind the steering wheel, the inside car temperature was almost warm. The sun shone bright, and there wasn't a cloud in the sky. Days like this always made me think of my blue-eyed soldier boy.

When I learned he'd passed away, I felt as if I'd died a thousand deaths. On the news, I learned of a Vietnam vet body found dead from exposure on the steps of the veteran's facility. It was Mike. My baby soldier boy. I'd had trouble keeping him from my mind ever since I learned of the situation and circumstances surrounding his death, which happened nine years ago. I needed to know more about him to help me put my mind at rest. I needed to know why.

My favorite drive-thru wasn't far. It didn't take long to receive my purchased order. The first taste of coffee brought a smile to my lips and the aroma assisted in opening my eyes wider. I turned toward the highway, eventually merging in with the traffic driving toward the downtown area.

Skyscrapers clouded the beautiful sunlight. Honking horns and cars jutting in and out kept me on edge since I wasn't used to driving in a larger metro area. The traffic made me nervous. City transit buses blocked corners and seemed to take up the road. I found the hospital parking ramp and eventually parked. When I finished my roll, I locked up behind me and walked toward the escalator, which brought me to the hospital door entrance.

My grandparents had died five years apart in the same hospital, many years ago. Bittersweet memories flooded my mind as my feet tapped their way toward the main desk. Soon, I was on the elevator and punching the right floor button. As the doors opened, I stared straight ahead at the nurses' station. Since a nurse looked right at me, I asked, "How is Judy Hokstad?"

"You are?"

"Nancy Bjork." My heart leaped into my throat when she raised a brow. It was the same look I'd seen when my parents died.

"Let me see—" She peered down at the desk monitor. "She's eating at the moment. I'm sure she'd be happy to see you. Her room is right down the hallway."

"Thank you," I said, smiling.

I followed her directions and easily found the room. The door stood slightly open, which gave me a chance to peek inside without being seen. Still dark hair but very pale. Thin came to mind. Her long, pointed nose caused me to grin from a sudden memory. Someone had closed a door on it once, and she had two black eyes for a long time, which wasn't much different than her present look.

"Get in here," Judy said. "I can't speak much louder, so hurry up!"

"You look ready for prom," I said. "Feelin' all right?"

"Just peachy. Couldn't be any better unless you offer me a stiff one." Judy raised a brow and said, "This is the last straw. I'm going for treatment, and don't say it's about time."

"Treatment? For what? Drinking? Explain."

"Oh, you know—drinking, marijuana, that sort of thing. The picture is a vista, not worth copying. My habitual drinking and driving. Having the insurance rates skyrocket. My department chair telling me I'm too old and smart for this kind of bullshit. The usual."

"You're tired of lectures? Like—'cut this shit out!' Is this what you're saying?"

"Yep."

"Good! Now, tell your older than snot girlfriend what happened."

"First off, my heater went on the blink and the gasses landed on the windshield, clouding it up. The inside was like looking through dark sunglasses."

"Oh dear God," I said. "When can you leave this popcorn stand?"

"I'll be able to get out this afternoon because the doctor is tiring of my sick jokes," Judy said, cocking her head. "Actually, I had a slight concussion plus the bruising. I should be able to check out by two, but I'm sure that charges will be filed."

"Most likely. I'm here for you. And any

convalescence you're staying at my house. I'll drive you around to the doctor and eventually dump you at the airport or escort you home."

"Yes, Sergeant-at-Arms," Judy said. "I've always been able to count on you."

"Remember that. I can't possibly know what's happening all the time when you're in a different state. We must keep in touch. Got it?"

"Got it."

"We're spending the night at Sharon's."

"I almost forgot, glad you reminded me," Judy said. "Sorry, never mind me, I'm not up to speed yet. I need about ten cups of coffee. I don't have any idea about my car. I don't know where my belongings or anything are. So Missy, I take it that you're my chauffeur? You'll pick me up and then take me to the impound lot? I'd be really grateful."

"Better call your insurance agent, too."

"He'll probably have a stroke over this. Five times in five years. Pretty good record, don't you think? I'm also thinking a lawyer is probably in order," Judy said.

"Make the calls right away this morning," I said.

"Actually, now that I think about it," Judy began, "let me give you the code for the car door, make, and model. When I find out for sure where it's located, then will you go and try to get my personal items?"

"Sure. I'll go right from the funeral and then come back here. It'll be late morning, early afternoon, I suspect."

"Sounds good. I'll get the doctor to let me out of this popcorn stand early. I'll tell him the food sucks and the service stinks. Hand me a paper and pen," Judy said.

"I'll grab whatever I can." I waited as she wrote the information. "I'd better get going. I don't want to be late."

"I wish this had never happened," Judy said, shaking her head.

"Me too," I said. I leaned over and kissed her forehead. "I love you."

"You too," Judy said.

I turned and left.

The clock behind the nurse as I stepped into the elevator read 9:00. I had just enough time to get across town and in the church before the service started.

Really, it was refreshing to see the Minneapolis skyline and all the new skyscrapers. I'd always loved going to the different schools for teacher workshops and going to eat in the downtown area. Paul never liked doing what I enjoyed, but he had his friends and clubs that took him away from me, which was too often. I wondered if he'd been dating behind my back?

Luck was on my side and so was the light Saturday morning traffic. I parked right on the button. I sent a message to Sharon as I climbed from the car and locked it. It read: *here*. Clutching my purse, I hurried as fast as I could on the slippery walkway to the church front doors and scooted inside. I opened the sanctuary doors and peered in. Mary sat on the edge near the front and waved me onward. I hurried and sat right beside her.

"I motioned to Sharon to hold off," she whispered.

"Thanks," I replied and clutched her warm hand.

After the first hymn, "Beautiful Savior," my mind was focused. I let my thoughts about Judy go for the moment and switched all my focus onto Margo and Sharon's comforting sermon about her life. Sharon spoke about Margo's early life and growing up in south Minneapolis, attending Julia Ward Howe Grade School, Maria Sanford Junior High and then Theodore Roosevelt High School. How she'd always dreamed of being an actress in New York but never had the opportunity. About her daughter, Mary, the one true joy in her life, and her job as a secretary at a nearby grade school.

Sharon welcomed Margo's old school chums, using our names, and thanked her fellow coworkers for attending. Because of the inclement weather, all were invited to the cemetery for burial but whoever cared to stay behind was welcome to have a cup of coffee while they waited for family and friends to return. A lunch in Margo's honor afterward would be served. The congregation sang, "How Great Thou Art," and then followed the procession from the sanctuary.

"Can I ride with you?" I asked.

"Sure, there is plenty of room in the limo."

"Thanks. I'm so sorry. I loved your mom."

"We all did," Mary said, blinking back tears.

"Ready?" Sharon said, coming up to us.

"We're all going to ride together. That's okay, isn't it, Sharon? I mean Reverend."

"Sharon." She gave Mary a hug, "I'm really sorry

about this."

"I feel miserable," I stated. "I wish we could have had one more time together."

"You and me both," Sharon replied. "Let's get into the limo."

"Yeah, we'll squeeze together into the back," Mary said.

"Yes, and I want to hear about Judy. You won't mind, will you, Mary?"

"I need the distraction to make it through the day," Mary replied.

The driver parked in the designated area near the lake inside of Lakewood Cemetery.

Sharon performed the graveside service. Afterward, one by one we strolled past the coffin. A few people left long stem roses. I left a light blue ribbon Margo and I had shared one summer. Sharon, a candle. Suddenly I thought of Judy and what she'd like to leave as a keepsake for her old friend. I removed a tube of red lipstick and smeared it thick on my lips, took out a blank sheet of paper, and kissed it. Next, I wrote, "From Judy," on it, then placed it on the coffin. At the last minute, Mary removed a purple ribbon and placed it on the coffin. Sharon nodded approval.

"I would, if I could," Sharon said. "That was sweet." She looked away.

The small crowd meandered away, and we turned to each other.

"It really was," I agreed. "Purple ribbon?" I glanced at Mary. "You aren't, are you?"

"Mom would have loved it and yes I am gay to answer your question."

"I'm happy that you've come to terms with your sexuality."

"Margo is with us, and looking down smiling, I know it," Sharon said. "Let's get going because I'm needed back at church, you two munchkins."

"You're right," I said, opening the car doors. We climbed into our respective places and buckled our seat belts.

"Do you need help with anything?" I asked Mary.

"Nope. I lived with Mom after I lost my job. She never commented on my choice of a partner. The very first time I hugged and kissed a woman in front of her, she gave us each a warm hug."

"Your mom was special." I touched her shoulder. "She was fun to be around. She was very kind and graceful. She was poor like the rest of us, but happy with what she had. I really loved her."

"Was your friend at the funeral?" Sharon asked.

"No, she wasn't. Her place of work wouldn't give her the day off because we're 'not married' even though we had a celebration of love and said our vows. I'll move in permanently with Laurie. We're looking forward to our time together. I'm going to our place when I leave the church."

"You carry a heavy load," I said. "You have my prayers."

"You've got a tough road to follow. Living the lifestyle of a homosexual isn't an easy one," Sharon said. "I'm right by your side—on the same path as you. I'm always willing to lend an ear if needed."

"Life can be tough, but prayers and good friends are some of the keys to happiness," I said, suddenly pale. Even though I was surprised, my heart ached for her. I also wondered how Mike would've accepted this knowledge about his favored sister. "Now, I'm concerned about Judy."

"Me, too. She's got an awful lot to sort through," Sharon said.

"Amen to that."

"How did Judy look?" Mary asked.

"Pale. I think she was nervous, and that's why she drank. But aren't we all?" I said. "It's such a shame that a funeral brought us together."

"Yes, it is," Mary said. I watched her rake her fingers through her hair. "It's a dirty shame that you girls couldn't have spent more time together. I know Mom would've loved it. She missed you all."

"Your mom raked her fingers through her hair when she was tired or anxious, just like you just did," I said.

"You're right, Mary," Sharon said. "We are all in agreement. Right?"

"Most certainly," I said. "I put together a wand or memory stick of some of my old pictures for you as a remembrance. I plan to add a few of Judy's. Do you mind if I work on it over the weekend?"

"Sure. Thanks, Nancy. Now I know why Mom missed you so much," Mary said. "You're very sweet."

"Nancy, it's good you are doing that," Sharon said.

The driver turned right near the church parking lot. "I'm glad we're all going to be together."

"What exactly did Margo die from?" I asked. "It was breast cancer, wasn't it?"

"Yes," Mary said. She raised her chin. "I'm to make you all promise to get mammograms, got it?" She sniffled.

"I love the sensation of being squished once a year," Sharon said. "I'm getting flattened top and bottom. It won't be long before my breasts look like pancakes."

"Mine are just as they should be," I said. "Thank heavens."

"Mary? You take doubly good care of yourself and don't worry about us," Sharon said, unlocking her seatbelt. "You're a beautiful woman and have many years ahead of yourself. And if you ever need me for anything, call."

"I will," Mary said. She wiped her eyes and blew her nose as Sharon climbed from the vehicle.

The little church was over a hundred years old, and it was built by Swedish immigrants during the beginning of the 1900s. The first church became too small, so in the mid 1950s a new church was built on the corner lot where it now stood. The neighborhood at one time was populated mostly by Scandinavians, and now it was filled with new inhabitants of Spanish, Hmong, or Somalian descent. All three of us girls grew up near here and were confirmed in this church.

We went to hang up our coats.

A familiar looking elderly woman who reminded

me of my mother, struggled with removing coat from over her shoulders, so I assisted.

She smiled. I returned the smile but kept going with Mary, realizing I hadn't paid Mom a visit for a few days. But, who was that woman?

Nancy
Chapter Four

I was happy when the luncheon finished. Sharon looked after her "flock," and I started toward the door but was stopped by the same older, frail woman.

"Hello. May I speak to you for a moment?"

"Sure. You're awfully familiar, but I can't place you," I said.

"I'm Vicky Storbaekkene's mother," she said. "Now, I finally see a glimmer in your eye. You're Nancy. You were always so kind and well-mannered. Vicky loved playing with you."

"Oh dear me! Vicky was such a good friend. I loved her dearly. In fact, I was just thinking about her and your family. I wish we knew what happened to her." I hugged her tight. "I am so sorry for not recognizing you. I should've. I apologize."

"Accepted. The funeral must've been hard for you?"

"I really do miss Vicky." Tears filled my eyes, and I wiped them dry with a tissue. "I came across a few pictures lately with her in them, they're from birthday parties."

"I'd like to see them," Mrs. Storbaekkene said.

"Have there been any new leads?"

"No, and that's another reason for coming to the

funeral, to speak to a friend of my daughter's. I hoped it would be you. Sharon, of course, wouldn't remember or know her from grade school like you or Judy. Where is Judy?"

"She was in the car crash that was on the news last night. I saw her this morning, and I think she'll be able to leave the hospital today."

"Good. Do you think you can give me your phone number? I'd like to speak with the three of you about my daughter." Mrs. Storbaekkene removed her phone from her purse. "My son told me I have to have this with me at all times, if I don't, he'll lock me in my room. That's what he told me." She grinned. "Call me Diane."

"Okay. I don't have children, but friends of mine say the same kind of stuff about theirs. A teacher friend was told by her oldest son that if she stayed out too late, she'd be grounded." I took out my phone, and we both added our numbers into our personal contact lists.

"Thank you. Do you mind if I call you later?" She cocked her head. "My son will bring me over, he said. Will. You remember him, don't you?"

"Of course, and I think I remember Vicky calling him Olaf sometimes?"

"That is his actual name. He's named after my dad but we call him Will. He never liked Olaf so he's always been Will. Only Vicky could call him that. He had a tender heart for her," Diane said. "Let me know about this evening."

"I will, but I must consult Sharon since we're

having a sleepover at her house tonight."

"I'll wait for your call."

"Good."

I gave her another hug and kiss on the cheek before she strolled away.

I sighed as she walked away, feeling totally heartbroken for her, for myself, and the whole darn day. I wished I wasn't here for Margo's funeral. I wished she was still alive and walking among us. Couldn't it have been someone else?

Sharon stopped me and said, "The older woman who you were speaking with looked awfully familiar."

"Vicky's mom and she wants to speak to all of us. I'm getting ready to go after Judy."

"Let's see how Judy is but how about inviting Mrs. Storbaekkene over later?" Sharon said. "She hasn't had closure and we have those pictures of yours and Judy's."

"We have made tentative plans to that effect, but I haven't had a chance to catch you up on them. It sounds as if her son, Will, might be able to bring her over in the later afternoon. I thought after we're all settled in." I gave it a moment's thought. "I bet she needs someone other than Will to speak to about Vicky."

"I'll see you later. I'm going to talk to Mary and a few other people. The key is under the flowerpot if you're there before me."

"Okay."

As I headed for the car, I thought about Vicky once

again. I buckled up and gave Judy a call. She answered almost immediately.

"Judy, you didn't tell me where the impound lot is, do you know?"

"I believe it's out Cedar Avenue and in Richfield. You can find it behind that garage where we used to go and flirt with those guys when we'd stop to fill up after going to Southdale."

"You flirted. Okay. Now I know where it's at," I said. "You ready to get out?"

"Pretty soon," Judy said. "I sure outdid myself."

"Honey, you're known for it."

"See you."

I started the engine and soon was turning toward 42nd Street.

Before I knew it, I turned onto Cedar, heading toward downtown and the impound lot.

In just a few minutes, I was entering the door, taking a numbered ticket, and waiting in line.

"Next!" the man exclaimed, turning over the number.

"Right here," I said. "I need to pick up the personal items from this vehicle." I showed him the make and model.

"Name?"

I swear the guy had so much hair sticking out of his ears it looked like bristles from a steel wool pad. His nose wasn't much better, and his eyebrows reminded me of a squirrel's tail. It was all I could do not to laugh.

"Nancy Bjork."

"Sign right here," he said, "but you can only look inside, can't take anything. It's an ongoing investigation."

"Okay, but what about her personal items? You know, her purse and suitcase?"

"Lady? I only know what I know," he said. He pushed the paper and placed his thick finger on the marked line. He clamped his jaw tight and stared at me. "Well?"

I signed my name. Soon I walked through the doors to the outside and easily found Judy's car. The roof was smashed down, the engine hood mangled, and the side window broken. Totaled. Fortunately, she'd worn her seatbelt or she would be in worse shape. I breathed in deeply and said a silent prayer, thanking God she was basically okay, then opened the door.

I looked through the car windows and into the front seat. It was full of papers from a drive thru. The back door was sort of sprung open, and I saw her makeup kit. I decided to try and sneak it out. Everyone needs makeup, I reckoned. I smiled once it was out and in my possession.

I traipsed to my car and placed the makeup case in the backseat. After climbing in and buckling up, I started the engine and was soon heading to the hospital.

I turned and parked in the hospital front lot. I soon walked into the main front doors. Since I knew the room number, I didn't make the usual information desk inquiry.

"Hey you," Judy said.

"I'm not sure what to say, but you look better than you did this morning." She looked too good for living through such an awful accident. Her pixie-cut brown hair was cute, her brown eyes looked tired and worn, but her smile brightened the room. As usual. "You look just as expected, colorful from the bruises."

"Always the charmer," Judy said. "Don't you like the different shades of blue?"

"Honey, it's no different than when you fell ice skating that time. Or what about bike riding?" I said, chuckling.

"How do you remember that? It must've been back in my growing stages. I always made a mess of myself. I looked like one of those kaleidoscope toy things. You remember those? You twist them around and different shades appear."

"You need to take better care of yourself."

"I'll try, but it ain't easy," Judy said. She rolled her eyes.

"I mean it. A shrink."

"Give me a hug, you little brat, but be careful, I'm still sore," Judy said.

"Oh, all right." I leaned in to her and hugged her. "You're a pain."

"I know." She pressed the buzzer and soon an attendant appeared with the wheelchair. "Let's go." She sat down in the chair.

"You two known each other a long time?" the attendant asked.

"You betcha," Judy responded.

"What does the doctor say?"

"I have to hang around a few days. I have a doctor's appointment Wednesday." She glanced at me and smirked.

"My pleasure. Your bed's all freshened up."

"I knew it. Nancy, you're too sweet. I'm covered in sugar."

"You're impossible. I'll get the car."

It didn't take long before I parked in front of the main door to wait for Judy. She arrived almost at the same time.

In a few minutes, I had Judy tucked inside of the car and buckled. I hurried around to the driver's side and quickly got inside. The engine was still running and it was toasty warm as I buckled myself into the seat.

"Here's your makeup. They wouldn't let me take anything out of the car." I handed it to Judy. "I sneaked this out."

"Thanks. The authorities probably want to search the car." Judy took it. "My license is revoked, too."

"Figures," I said. "We'll have to fly you home."

Judy nodded.

"Tell me what they'll find in the car," I said.

"An empty flask, but the best and worst incrimination is right here in this bag. Thank God for small favors," Judy said.

"What is it?" I asked.

"Never mind. We're off. What's Sharon serving up besides God and goodness?" Judy reached out her hand and said, "How about a smoke?"

"No one else can smoke in the car, but I'll let you, if you roll the window down."

"Thanks. I desperately need one," Judy said. "Are we driving past the house?" She partially rolled her window down before lighting her cigarette. She took a drag and blew it out of the window opening.

"Of course. It's for sale, and I want to see it. I haven't been in the neighborhood for ages."

"You maybe haven't, but Mike is still on your mind. If he wasn't, you wouldn't be driving past his house."

"Be quiet," I said. "I have good memories of our time together."

"You need to move on. Get remarried."

"I'm not ready for that. It was tough splitting with Paul. Now he has a family and seems happy. I'm finally happy now, too."

"No, you're not. I can see it in your eyes," Judy said. "I'm not either."

"It's about time you admitted that."

"We're getting to the bottom of all of our secrets this weekend, come hell or high water," Judy said. She took another long drag, then shoved the remaining cigarette out of the window before rolling it up once again.

It wasn't long before I turned onto Lake Street, then 42nd Avenue. Driving along, we passed the coffee shop, parking on a side road.

"There it is," I said. The For Sale sign stuck out like a sore thumb. "This kills me, really. I remember going inside and meeting Mike's mother, sisters, and dad.

The whole family. I was scared to death, but Mike was attentive. He could read in me that I was ready to flee. His arm on my shoulder, holding my hand, settled me down. We sat side by side on the couch while his mom showed me pictures from his baby album. I only wish I knew why he told me to forget about him."

"Still your passion?" Judy asked. She squeezed my shoulder. "Not knowing why he split must be rough. Is this why you can't let him go?"

"It's awful to go through life wondering," I said. "Maybe Sharon will shed some light on it."

"I can only hope. She hasn't been very forthcoming over the years, has she?" Judy said.

I drove away from the curb, merging in with the traffic.

Suddenly, there was too much silence in the car. It gave the drive an eerie feeling. Looking over at Judy, I noticed her biting her lower lip. Whenever she did that, I knew to hang onto my boots. She was about ready to say something that would surprise the heck out of me. I took a deep breath to prepare myself because the blast was soon to arrive.

"Something happened to me one night, and we need to talk about it. We were all at the party when the hockey team arrived. Tonight, I want to discuss it," Judy said. "There's always hope we can face our secrets and we can become close once again." She lit another cigarette.

"Secrets?" I said. "I don't have any."

"We all have something hidden in our hearts that hasn't been exposed. It's time to let it all out."

"Doctor Judy needs to let sleeping dogs lie," I said. "My secrets lay hidden in this house and the one we're staying at tonight. Sharon has mine tucked in her heart, but her lips are zipped tight. What are yours?"

"Later."

"By the way, Vicky Storbaekkene's mom and brother plan to stop over later today. She wants to see us and, it's my guess, discuss what's happened to the investigation."

"All right," Judy said. "The pictures, right?"

"Yes, I told her about them." I glanced her way. "I remember copying Vicky's math problems during tests so I could at least pass. She stole a few of my language answers. Boy, she was smart."

"She sure was. Science, she was the whiz kid. Without her, I never would've been able to dissect the frog. Remember that?"

"Yes, and I hated it!" I drove up 38th Street, turning onto 35th Avenue and parked. The lights lit up the entryway. Sharon greeted us with a big smile, hugs, and kisses. "Secrets should remain secret," I said.

"It's too late."

Judy
Chapter Five

When Margo passed away, I hoped for closure to both Nancy and Sharon, especially Nancy. Sharon owed her a lot. I wasn't privy, of course, to why Mike had broken the engagement. Mike never admitted he didn't love Nancy, which was why she probably could never let him go in her heart and move on with her life. Secrets and more secrets. Sharon should've known better.

Friends and acquaintances died every day, but Margo's death hit like a thunderbolt. She knew all my secrets, such as cheating in school and telling the teacher that Dougie swiped my answers and he was the cheater. Bless her pea-picking heart.

"By jove! Here we are! Nothing's changed, and I bet the furniture is about identical to everyone else in this neighborhood," I said.

"Judy, you need to tame it down a notch. This funeral is hard on all three of us," Nancy said. She parked.

"Yes, Miss Minnesota Nice, I'm trying."

Just as I opened my door, Sharon rushed from the house to gather me into her arms.

"You're beautiful, Judy, I'm glad that you're here." She almost crushed me to pieces as I broke into tears.

After Nancy joined in on the hug-crusher, she carried her small bag inside, saying she'd return for her albums.

"I'm so glad we're together again." Sharon gave us each another big hug and took our coats to hang in the entryway closet. "This is too late in coming."

"Oh, Sharon, I love you," I said and wiped my eyes. "I made such a mess out of this. I wanted to be there with you."

"Honey," Sharon said, "you were there in spirit, and besides, Nancy placed a mushy kiss on a piece of paper and set it on the coffin for you. Now you're here with us."

I looked at Nancy and smiled. "You didn't tell me."

"Nope. I was in the moment," Nancy said. She winked at me. "Cool, eh?"

"You still have the moves, girl," I said.

"Judy, what do you care to drink?" Nancy asked. "There are sodas. As a matter of fact, why don't I have one?"

"Nothing for me except water," I said. "I took a few over-the-counter pills, that's all that was prescribed. It's only for headaches because of the mild concussion." I opened my makeup kit, removing my cigarettes. "Mind?"

"Please, not in the house. I have asthma," Sharon said. "I've been hospitalized because of attacks. They're awful."

"I'm sorry. I didn't know," I said, setting the pack aside.

"It's been a rough day and a soda would hit the spot," Sharon said.

"Here's the sodas and water for Judy," Nancy said. She carried three filled glasses on a tray.

"I'm exhausted," Sharon said. "I'm suddenly really tired." She plunked into the nearest recliner chair and shut her eyes.

"Sharon? Don't you feel well?" Nancy asked.

"Give me ten."

Almost instantly, we heard a soft snore from Sharon's direction. Nancy and I smiled at each other and nodded toward the old phonograph in the corner.

"Time to snoop!" Nancy said. "Where to begin?"

"Let's play them," I said.

Sharon woke to the two of us standing by the closet, snooping through old records. "I've kept them all," she said. "I even have the first Beatles."

"Wow!" I held up *Meet the Beatles*.

"Oh! You're up," Nancy said. "Judy and I opened a bag of nacho chips and found dip." Nancy dipped another chip, popping it into her mouth.

"Fine by me," Sharon said.

Sharon went over to the phonograph and opened the lid. "Let's stack 'em up, ladies."

"Now, I'm not feeling the greatest," I said. "Mind if I take over Sharon's spot, anyone?"

"Go ahead," Nancy said.

Soon Nancy and Sharon were hopping and be-bopping to our favorite cherished musicians of the sixties: Bob Dylan, Mamas and Papas, Peter, Paul and Mary, Simon and Garfunkel, plus other bands such as

Creedence Clearwater Revival. As I snoozed for ten minutes, I knew Sharon would dance around Nancy and she'd scoot around her.

"Ain't we cool?" I asked. "Look at you two busting a move!" I opened my eyes just as they plopped down on the nearest chairs.

"Do you remember Home Ec and making those silly, checkered aprons?" Nancy asked.

"Yeah! And then wearing them when we cooked," I said. "Red. That's me."

"I had blue. The color of Mike's eyes," Nancy said.

"Whatever happened to Miss Olson? Anyone know? Besides sewing, she taught cooking," I said.

"She fell off the planet," Nancy said. "Vanished." She snapped her fingers. "Miss Olson in zipper heaven surrounded by gingerbread houses no one wants to eat."

"She tasted my dish of macaroni and cheese, and I thought her eyes would float to the back of her head, that she'd be permanently cross-eyed," I said.

"She made me rip out the seams on a skirt five times. Five times! I threw it away. She was mean," Nancy said.

"Let's bow our heads and close our eyes and pray the Lord's Prayer for Miss Olson so she can find peace wherever she is," Sharon said.

We shut our eyes, folded our hands as Sharon led the prayer.

When finished, time stood still while we gathered our thoughts.

"That was a good thing to do," Nancy said.

"Yes, it was," I said.

"What color was your apron?" Nancy looked at Sharon.

"I never sewed one. In my school, we made dishcloths," Sharon said.

"Dishcloths? If you have one, you'll have to bring it out and show it," Nancy said.

"My word! I got rid of it a long time ago."

"Whatever happened to those aprons?" I asked.

"No clue," Nancy said. "Lost, but not forgotten."

"Never forgotten all those lovely brownies and vanilla puddings we made during our birthday overnights," I said.

"Saturday afternoon we'd walk to the Riverview Theater or else go downtown and look around. We'd never have any money except to buy a Coke and a hotdog at Woolworths' counter," Nancy said.

"These songs, the three of us together, man it sure brings back the memories. I think we should sit down and talk. Get to know each other again," I said.

"Good thought," Sharon said. "Where should we begin?"

"Our lives. How we ended up doing what we do for a living and what's happened to us over the years," I said. "We all have hidden secrets or treasured moments. Let's do it."

"First off, let's all tell why we are here?" Nancy said.

"Margo, of course," I said.

"Why else? What are you getting at?" Nancy said.

"You're all skirting the issues," I said and reached

for the pack of smokes, removing one. I slipped it back into the pack. "Sorry, Sharon."

"Listen Judy, we have more important issues to concern ourselves with than bringing up past stories. We have photos to go through and a memory stick to make for Mary. She deserves a keepsake from us as a remembrance for her mom," Nancy said.

"There's also the issue about Vicky's mom, Diane," Sharon said.

"I forgot."

"I have Diane's number and planned to arrange it," Nancy said. "No facing demons tonight, at least not until after they leave."

Sharon crossed her arms and said, "And that's the way that it is."

"If you say so Mother Theresa," I said.

"I do."

Nancy whipped out her phone and placed the call.

"They'll be here shortly. Will lives nearby and Diane is in the same home where Vicky grew up. She's never moved," Nancy said. She shrugged.

"I wonder what there is to talk about? Any new leads?" I said. "My brain is half-fried. I wouldn't know a porcupine from an elephant at the moment."

It was going to be a very long night.

While we waited, I went outside to have a smoke. The cigarette sure tasted good. I'd thought about quitting for a long time—who didn't these days? Someday, I would. I decided that after this accident, it was time to quit drinking. Maybe once the truth all came out and this dirty, nasty, awful feeling went away I could.

As I zipped open the inside secret pocket of my makeup kit where I'd stored my last joint, I sighed. I'd forgotten about smoking it. I hoped it had been a good one because I knew that I'd never have another. Those days were done. Gone. Kaput!

A squirrel busied itself on the edge of the deck and soon scampered up the nearest tree, a sure sign of winter. It was a bit brisk out, so I snuffed out the last of my smoke and headed back inside. It was time to scoot through the albums.

"I'm starved. That hospital food wouldn't keep critters alive."

"You're hilarious sometimes, Judy," Sharon said. "I love you for that."

They sat side-by-side looking through photo albums. I found a small container of potato salad, fork and went to slide in beside them on the couch.

"Oh my, Judy," Nancy said. "Look what you have in your album, Miss Smartie-pants." She removed the picture from the album and held it up for us to see. "Guess who that is?"

"The four of us playing dress-up!" I said and grinned. "Look at wobbly Margo. She looks like a Christmas tree with her red, curly hair and the long green dress."

"Definitely add," Sharon said. "Mary's gonna love it. Look at that one." She pointed to the photo on the following page. "Tell me about this picture. You're lined up in a row, the four of you."

"Oh! Look! Here we are fixing each other's hair.

Look at us! Trying on the dresses to see who looked better in which dress! Those were the days!" Nancy said.

"This one, here," I pointed at it, "is definitely prom night. Larry, Moe, and Curly locks," I said. "Vicky dressed in pink. You sure know who Curly is with the red hair."

"I wonder if Vicky's mom has a copy of this one?" Nancy said. She pulled it out from the album and held it up.

"I must've taken the picture," Sharon said. "It wasn't prom night for me, and I didn't go, anyway. My partner had flown the coop."

"Yeah, and my partner was in Vietnam so he'd flown the coop, too!" Nancy suddenly became teary-eyed. She wiped them dry. "I'm so sorry. Don't mind me." She blew her nose.

The doorbell rang, and Sharon went to answer it.

Vicky's mother and brother entered. She looked just as imagined, and he looked worn from worry. I didn't think it was the snowball effect of the mom that made her look older, either, I believed it was caused from the wear and tear of wondering what happened to her daughter. He was turning gray like the rest of us, had a paunch but seemed like he had a heavy heart. I felt for them.

Sharon had them take a seat after introductions were made.

"Will, Mrs. Storbaekkene, Nancy and Judy," Sharon said.

"Call me Diane."

"Diane, ever since you told me that six cookies and three chocolate covered donuts were enough, that one day way back when, you've been on my list." I grinned. "Will? It's good to meet you again."

"I agree," Will said. He looked at Nancy.

"I remember Vicky calling you Olaf sometimes. I can see why you like Will better," Nancy said.

"I didn't like being called Ollie or Olaf the loafer. I had a fit and insisted on Will sometime around third grade. Vicky quit calling me that as she grew older." He smiled. "It's good to be here and meet my sister's friends once more."

"I've missed you girls something fierce," Diane replied. "You've been especially high on my list. How are you? Before we begin talking about my daughter, I'd like to know what you three Barbie Dolls have been up to?" She chuckled. "Go on, now Judy, speak up."

"I've a doctorate in German studies and teach in Madison. No children, thank God. Married and divorced. He didn't like the German I used on him so much!"

"You should've known to curse in English, then he would've liked it," Nancy said with a grin.

"We're still good friends," I said. "He's always checking up on me."

"Good! Someone has to," Sharon said.

"Nancy?"

"I'm divorced and live in Linden. Teach. No children."

"Sharon, you're a wonderful minister and this is your house," Diane said. "It's beautiful."

"Hum," Will said. "Now that we've had introductions…"

"Right. Let's get down to brass tacks," I said. "Nancy found a couple pictures to show you."

"Yes. Here they are." Nancy handed them to her. "This is prom night, but you already know that by the dress and the background of Minnehaha Creek. These other photos, you've maybe not seen. We're playing dress-up and dolls, swimming, etc."

Diane and Will studied the pictures.

"My lovely daughter." Tears sprang into Diane's eyes. "These are lovely. Can I have a copy of each?"

"Of course!"

"I do miss my sister." Will glanced up at us. "We need to talk about the last place where she was seen, and this is it. What happened after the photo was taken? Such as, was there anyone hanging around? Did she mention anyone she might see later or was looking forward to meeting up with? We'd like to try and open the case. We need closure."

"Let me make a copy, hold on," Nancy said. She took a picture of the photos on her cell phone. "We're putting together a memory stick for Mary with photos of her mom." She handed the pictures back to Diane.

"Take them," I said. "You should have them."

"Thanks," Will said. "So, who took the snapshot at the creek before the dance?"

"I took it," Sharon said.

"She had two pictures left on the roll of film, I remember," Nancy said. "I was there but didn't go to prom."

"So, we have Judy, Margo, and Vicky photographed."

"Ahh, you're wondering what escapades happened directly thereafter," I said. "My boyfriend awaited in the chariot back at the parking lot for me and Margo."

"Vicky's boyfriend, who was it?" Nancy said. "I don't remember."

"Why didn't Vicky ride with you two?" Sharon said. "I don't remember."

"We didn't want so many kids in the same car because of prom night. Safety first, you know? Drinking and driving," Diane said. She had a faraway look in her eyes.

"Steve Turner. He'd been a good friend of mine," Will said. "He testified they'd gone to the prom. He lived across the street and a block away from the park at the time. They'd met up right after the pictures were taken. He would've been there for the picture taking, but his mom had him change a lightbulb for her before he could leave."

"It checked out?" I said.

"Yes. The police searched his house, car, everything. No evidence of any wrongdoing."

"I assume that you've retraced her steps?" Sharon asked.

"Many times. Forward and back," Diane said.

"This necklace was found on the ground near the old Soldier's Home," Will said.

"Let me see it," Nancy said. She thoroughly studied it and opened the heart clasp, revealing a tiny picture of Steve."

"I don't know what to say, but I really feel terrible about her disappearance." I took the necklace from Nancy and held it tightly. "They checked it for fingerprints, I take it?"

"Yes," Will said.

"She went to prom, and they went to make-out down by the old Soldier's Home afterward? Correct?" Sharon said. She looked from Diane to Will. "It all seems odd that more clues haven't resurfaced. She never returned home, right?"

"No. Steve testified that he was attacked. When he woke, she was gone."

"I assume he went to the police?"

"The following afternoon when we couldn't locate her."

"Where is my beautiful daughter? What happened to her? I want to know before I die." Diane's eyes filled with tears. She blew her nose.

"Our Lord is keeping her safe, Diane," Sharon said. She placed a hand on her head and whispered a silent blessing.

"Mom, the girls will help. Won't you?"

"Yes, of course. I have a diary at home somewhere that I'll go through," Nancy said.

"I'll see if I can dig up anything in old records from the Home or possibly do a follow up in our church records."

"I knew you girls would help us out," Diane said. "Thank you."

"Steve Turner is still in Minneapolis, I'm almost

certain of it." Will removed his phone and tapped a couple of buttons and said, "Here's my number." When we'd copied it into our phones and added Diane's, he slipped his phone back inside of his pocket. "Mom?"

"Time to go," Diane said. "Thank you."

"Wait a second," Sharon said. She said a prayer over Diane and Will. "Peace be with you, and trust that we'll bring new light and clues to the authorities soon."

"Yes, give us time to look through our stuff."

"If it's any consolation," I said, "she was wonderful. Without her, I never would've made it through math or science. She always let me cheat. She was a good person and friend and took great pity on me and my intelligence."

Diane chuckled and gave us each a cheek kiss before leaving. We watched as Will assisted his mother into the car and drove away.

I turned to Nancy and Sharon.

Within seconds, we had a group hug.

Nancy
Chapter Six

"That was a blow to the heart," I said. I blew my nose. "I sure feel for them. They're still hurting."

"They need closure," Sharon said. "I'll hustle over to the old Soldiers' Home on Monday. Few people will be around so I'll be able to take my time. They'll let me peruse the indexes. I've been there many times searching for family records for parishioners who've wondered about former family members."

"How will you know where to begin or what to look for?" Judy said. "I wish there was more to go on, like the abductor's dirty socks or underwear."

"Let's be serious," Sharon said.

"I am and it's true. There's nothing to go on. No more clues. Nothing to trace Vicky with. It's like she vanished from the face of the earth and was never born!" Judy said.

"Judy? You need to put that brain of yours to rest. Take a pill or something," I said. "I have diaries at home that haven't been looked at for many years. Why I ever saved them is beyond me, but maybe this is the why? To help find Vicky."

"You're right."

"Let's pool our knowledge," Sharon said. She glanced at each of us. "We love each other and want the best for one another, but now we need to combine our talents to locating Vicky."

"You're right," I said. "I'm sorry, Judy. I sounded cross and mean, which I don't like to be. Let's get started."

"I developed a knack for seeing details in grad school grad school. I had to write tons of papers concerning Germany and never had the cash to travel back then so I made up everything from looking at pictures."

"I do have my diary but it's at home."

"Right. All three of us have a job to do," Sharon said, "and we can't get started until we are home or on Monday."

"For now," I said, "let's finish with this memory stick chore."

"What's left?" Judy said.

"Just these few from you," I said. "Give me a couple of minutes and I'll have it ready. I'll save it and make copies for us and give it to you later."

"Okay," Sharon said. "Judy? How about helping me get supper lined up?"

"I'm sorry for being a pill earlier, it's just that I'm beat. Really. I just want to rest."

"You must have a headache," I said. "Rest is the key word."

I made my way up the stairs to the spare room where all of my stuff was located. As I continued with copying the few pictures and adding them onto the correct spot, I heard music softly playing and clinking and clanking from the kitchen. I hoped Sharon hadn't gone to much trouble.

When finished, I brought the memory stick down to Sharon and held it up.

"Where should I put it?"

"Right here in this drawer. It might get lost in the drawer but won't get accidentally thrown away." Sharon removed a container from the microwave. "I wonder how Judy is?"

While I checked on Judy, she took care of the finishing touches for our meal.

"Judy? You waking?" I leaned into her. "Sweetie," I whispered, "are you hungry?" She opened one eye, then two, and shut them. "Well?"

"I suppose it's hot dishes from the funeral," Judy said. She kept her eyes closed. "I'm warm and comfy but feeling grumbles in my tummy."

"I'll bring you a plate. Stay put."

In the kitchen, I found Sharon placing macaroni and cheese on the table as well as a dish of leftover meatballs and gravy.

"I'm glad you're using paper plates. We can put the meatballs over a slice of bread," I said. "I'll dish up for Judy."

Sharon removed a stack of paper plates from the cupboard and plastic utensils.

I fixed up a small plate of food for Judy and carried it to her while Sharon took care of pouring us each a glass of milk. Once we'd settled in to eat in the living room, I smiled.

"This is just like old times, isn't it?"

"Yep. Me on the couch with a throbbing head, you

grinning over who knows what, and Sharon blessing us all. Couldn't be better!"

"You're hopeless," Sharon said. "Count your blessings and be happy that you're here."

"Yes! I love you Judy and Sharon. Now it's just us three."

"Thanks, but you make it sound like we're the last resort. Let's play remember when?" Judy said.

"Do we have to?" Sharon said.

"If you insist, but I'd rather eat in peace."

"No way anyone is getting out of this," Judy said. "Where did you have your first cigarette?"

"I have to think about that," Sharon said. "My mind isn't the same, you know? It's a little rusty."

"Honestly, Judy! It was at a Longfellow Park dance. Remember?" I said, blushing. "I shook like a leaf when I tried to light it." I took a bite of food from my plate.

"Nope, we'd piled into that car of Margo's and went to the drive-in." Sharon smiled at the memory. "It was so much fun." She kept eating. "I didn't realize I was so hungry!"

"*M*A*S*H*," I said. "That was a hoot!"

"Yeah, well, it was the weed that you remember, sweetie," Judy said. "I offered it to everyone in the car."

"Yikes!" Sharon said. "And now, the drug is ten-times stronger."

"Love it! What's next?" I said.

"Was it you that invited the entire Wobegon High School hockey team to the year end hockey party? The one after we went to state and beat the pants off of Warroad High School! The northern teams were always tough to score on." Judy looked at me.

"Oh! That one," Sharon said. "It was so long ago. Why bring it up?"

"The party was held at the clubhouse over by Nokomis. Remember? It's now a fitness center but back then, it was rented for any number of reasons. Our class raised funds to have a senior party in the building since we'd done so well in sports that year. All those rooms, up and down. I think some of the more well-to-do families donated to the event. It should've been fun," Judy said. She studied each of us. "Finally we're starting to open up. Who invited the hockey team?"

"I think they showed up on their own," Sharon said with a puzzled look.

"I didn't invite them." Cocking my head, I asked, "Who did?"

"Maybe I did," Sharon said thoughtfully. "I, ahh, invited the cheerleaders."

"Now we're getting somewhere," Judy said.

"We still don't know about the hockey team for sure. There were so many other classmates there, plus from Wobegon," Sharon said. "Where are you going with this, Judy? Whatever happened was so long ago, I don't remember much. I do know that a guy kissed me and I hated it, which is when I found out that I didn't like men."

"I wasn't there at all, but Judy? What happened to you?"

"What's bothering you, Judy?" Sharon asked. "There's something that isn't right and you're holding back on us. We need to know."

"If there's something that either one of us did to you, we want to know," I said. "Did anyone hurt you?"

"What about Margo? She was there, wasn't she? Was she kissed? By how many?" Judy asked.

"Judy's right. We need to talk," I said. "Judy is onto something. We must bring it out into the open."

"Sharon, I had sort of a suspicion years ago when you were younger and ignored boys. We haven't seen much of each other so there's nothing I can pinpoint, however, we love you for who you are," Judy said.

"Yes. Always loved you." We had another group hug. "Have you 'come out of the closet', as they say?"

"I do have a friend, but she's still married and looking for a divorce. She has a child. It's complicated." Sharon took a deep breath.

"The many Bible thumpers? How are they?"

"Don't know." Sharon shook her head and grabbed a tissue. "I'd probably be either kicked out of the church or sent to a small town faraway." She blew her nose. "However, I have thought about branching out and seeking a social worker degree or retire."

"Then for sure, I'll retire. Hands down! All three of us besties!" Judy said. "You betcha!"

"You might have to move to Minnesota," I said. "You know? For us besties to have fun together again."

"Oh dear God! Lutefisk!"

"You're a nut," Sharon said.

We giggled.

"Enough silliness. We need to focus on the present," I said.

"Ahh, Miss Innocent who spoons over a long lost lover and lives in the past but once had a husband who loved you. You could've had a family and been happy," Judy said. "You're the person who needs to focus on the present."

"Hey, you two!" Sharon said. "Let's bring this around to the here and now. Judy's hurting, and we need to get to the bottom of it and give her some love and comfort."

"You're right," I said and took a deep breath.

"This is exactly what I was getting at, ladies. We need to discuss a few matters," Judy said. She glanced from one person to another before continuing, "I was drugged."

"What?" Sharon said with her eyes open wider. "I didn't know."

"Drugged. I had gone upstairs to use the bathroom." Judy shuddered. When I came to, it was daylight." Tears flooded her eyes. "Why didn't someone come looking for me? Why not? I was deserted and left alone with no one to help. Not even to call a cab or walk me home. No one. Now start answering."

"Me?" I asked. "I didn't go to parties with different guys because I was engaged." I pulled Judy into my arms and kissed her cheek before releasing. "I'm so sorry, honey."

"Sharon? You brought over some friends of yours. Remember?"

"You poor thing, this is my fault. The cheerleaders must've invited their boyfriends to come and the list of guests multiplied," Sharon said, wrapping her arms around Judy. "I should've looked for you when you went missing. I had looked in the downstairs rooms but never thought of the upstairs." She softly hugged and smoothed her palm down Judy's back. "I'm so sorry. I should've looked harder." She sniffled.

"Forgive us, Judy, for not being there for you," I said. "We're such fools."

"I trusted you guys. You know? All for one and one for all?"

"I know. It's no excuse," Sharon said. "I had a terrible time that night, too."

Judy broke into tears.

"Let it all out, sweetie." I swept her up in my arms once again. "I'm so sorry Judy."

"You're so brave, Judy," Sharon said. "It was an awful night, but I'm glad now that you've been able to release your pain."

In silence, we sat, lost in thought. Afterward, I helped clean up the kitchen while Judy made herself ready for bed. She hadn't wanted any assistance but left the bathroom door unlocked in case she needed help for some reason.

Afterward, Sharon took care of her nightly routine while Judy lay on the couch. I spent the next few minutes looking around the living room and getting my bearings. I must admit, Sharon sure had old things. Not just records and albums, but a kerosene lamp, old china cabinet, an immigrant trunk that had rosemaling painted on it. I knew it had once belonged to her great-grandmother who traveled with it from Norway. She had crocheted doilies, which I assumed were from her grandmother or mother. The dishes in the cabinet had gold inlaid designs. I knew they also came from her grandmother.

Just as I wondered when Sharon would finish upstairs, she returned.

"Would you like a cup of hot tea?" Sharon said.

"Actually," I said. "I'm going to get comfy and will be right back."

"A cup of tea sounds good," Judy said. "It's comfy and cozy."

"I'll put the kettle on," Sharon said.

"Sharon, can I ask a favor? I think we're about the same size. I don't have any clothes with me, thanks to our lovely Minnesota weather."

"I'll set a nightie out for you on my bed and clothes for the next few days. I know you're at Nancy's so she can return them to me at a later date," Sharon said.

"Thanks."

"I'll have a cup when I return. Then I want you to tell me about Mike," I said.

"Here comes the beating of the drums," Judy said. "Well—Sharon?"

"I'll consider some of it. I did make a solemn oath to him before he died."

I glared at both.

Sharon looked away. Judy changed the subject.

"The crocheted throw looks homemade. The Terry Redlin print on the wall reminds me of up north and the lake. Warmth oozes from the room," I heard Judy say as I bounded upstairs and slipped into my jammies and robe.

It wasn't long before I'd taken care of myself and marched back down to the living room to find Judy staring at a wall hanging of a family picture.

I walked over to the picture. As I gazed at it, Sharon bumped my arm, "Nancy, you're in this, way back in the corner."

"Why did Mike break the engagement?" I continued studying the picture. Mike and I stood so close, not a breath of air could squeeze between us. "He was one handsome young man. I remember the picture being taken. He insisted I be in it." My eyes moistened, and I blinked them dry. "I was nuts over him. I guess I still am, in a way, to be honest."

"I'm so sorry Nancy, for love lost," Judy said. "Sharon tell her what you know. It's time to tell her why."

"Now. Truthfully. Right from the beginning to the end, that's how you'll do it," I replied. Sharon stared at the picture and held my hand.

"I'll be right behind you offering support," Judy said.

"It's hard to think of Mike as dead and then talk about it. He was my favorite brother. Phillip, my other brother, is quite a bit younger so I didn't know him as well growing up," Sharon said, taking a deep breath. "Let's sit for a minute and have our tea before going to bed."

"Then you'd better give me something, Sharon, or I'll leave."

"I hear the teapot whistling, I'll be right back with the cups," Judy said. "Now's your time to tell her Sharon, if you need privacy."

"I want to know the circumstances surrounding his death and why he cancelled the engagement."

"It's not that easy, Nancy. Suffice it to say, he did say you were the love of his life, but he swore me to secrecy about his illnesses. I've wrestled with the decision. This funeral of Margo's has hit us all pretty hard. Give me time. I haven't been through my mother's belongings. Let me do that first before I tackle the issue over Mike. Please do that for me," Sharon said. Tears sprang into her eyes and she dried them. "I'm sorry Nancy. I need time. I still can't believe he's dead and it's been nine years."

"Do you promise to tell me soon?"

"Yes. Just remember that you were the love of his life."

Judy entered with the hot tea.

"Better?" Judy asked.

"Barely."

After drinking my tea, I went upstairs.

As I tucked myself in, I wondered what other secrets lay within these house walls.

Judy
Chapter Seven

I was still snoring when Nancy walked down the hallway in the wee morning hours. I did hear the coffee perking and the refrigerator door opening and closing but never really came awake. I pulled the blankets up over me and went back to sleep. It was some time later, when the sun glared at me that I finally woke up.

"'Bout time," Nancy said. "Sharon got a call during the night from a parishioner and never returned. She's probably in church, getting ready for the sermon."

"I need coffee," I groaned. "My head hurts."

"Coffee and aspirin, coming right up. You can have that, can't you?"

"Yes, of course. Nothing else though. I'm not on any meds for illnesses but do have a few to help bring down the bruising."

"I'm proud of you," Nancy said. "Be right back." She took off for the kitchen, presumably to add some goodness to my coffee cup.

"I'm going upstairs. Don't expect to see the whites of my eyes for a while. I'm not moving too fast. I'm very stiff."

"My house doesn't have stairs." Nancy called from the kitchen.

"I'll remember that when I trip on a rug!"

I could see that I won't have a moments worth of peace while under her care. Miss Goodness, manifested. I went upstairs to dress, the grump, that I felt like. I really ached and hurt all over. Bruises had manifested themselves overnight. My arms, chest, and shoulders really were of the purple rainbow color, but not a deep color so the pills must be helping. My muscles and joints, and especially my back, hurt. Some of the aches and pains may well have been caused from sleeping on the couch. I wondered if that was a wise decision to choose it for overnight, but I thought I'd be less bothered during the night because of bathroom breaks and snoring.

True to form, Sharon had an array of clothes laid out on her bed. For today, I wore a loose fitted shift. It was easily gotten into and also wasn't tight across my shoulders. The sleeves were long, covering all my little indentations and flabby skin.

When I returned downstairs, Nancy was in the kitchen cooking up some eggs and bacon. I sat down by the kitchen table.

"I'll have one, and thanks." The coffee cup was filled and placed in front of me, which I immediately sipped. "This is delicious. I'll have to have a refill."

"Sure thing. How many eggs?"

"Two," I said. "I appreciate you doing this for me. You and Sharon. Don't say, 'all for one and one for all,' please. I'm ornery and cranky and not myself."

"You've had a tough time, Judy."

Nancy turned her back and continued cooking

breakfast.

"I'll take the bacon right away," I said. "It smells wonderful."

At that very moment, we both got a beep on our phones.

"It's Sharon," I said. "You must've gotten the same."

"Read it." Nancy removed the bacon onto a plate and set it before me.

Stuff keeps happening around here. After church, I have to go and visit an older woman in the nursing home to pray with the family. I'm so sorry. Take the clothes you need, Judy. Eat what you want. Please clean up. Love you both. We'll be in touch. Nancy, take care of our Judy. Sharon.

Thank you for everything.

"I sent her a message, thanking her for everything."

"I'll do the same, later. Let's eat," Nancy said. "We've been holding our own secrets for too long. Sharon has probably been afraid to talk about her sexual preference. I'd like to meet her friend. I should've said so."

"Me too. It might be possible before I leave for home."

Nancy served the fried eggs on individual plates before sitting down across from me. We ate them quickly.

"I feel like a queen. I feel like weight has been lifted from my shoulders," I said. "How about you?"

"I'm getting there," Nancy said. "At least I know I've been right all along. Mike did love me dearly and it sounds as if he never got over me either." Tears filled her eyes.

On my phone, I have a music app and turned on one of the stations. Lo and behold, it was playing one of our favorite songs. Soon we hummed the tune to "Puff the Magic Dragon."

"We're all guilty about this. Each and every one for not listening to each other's pain," Nancy said. "We're placed on this earth to help ease each other's burdens and suffering. We need to listen and love each other more."

"I agree."

"Hopefully, we've learned from the experience," Nancy said. "I stayed away from parties as much as possible. I worked extra hours to make the time go fast. I waited for my Mike." She sighed.

"True, we should try harder," I said. "I want to hear more about Margo."

"I can't get over that she's not here," Nancy said. "She had only Mary but never married. Odd, don't you think?"

"She was left alone so much to look after her younger brother. Her parents were away quite a bit for his job, leaving them alone. Her grandma looked in on them occasionally, but Margo basically raised her younger brother. When she was able, she moved out and fended for herself. Her younger brother Russ committed suicide when he was fifteen. She was alone until Mary, and the dad never stepped forward to help pay for her care or acknowledge that he had a baby girl. It was tough on Margo, but she managed."

"I never knew. My knowledge of her pretty much ends from the time I moved and started at the University of Madison."

"Margo went to secretarial school. Sharon and I visited her in the hospital when Mary was born. That's how we knew."

"I wish you'd told me." I reached for my coffee cup and realized the aspirins must've kicked in because I felt better or else it was the combination with the decent breakfast.

"Tell me what's going to happen with you now." Nancy poured herself another cup of coffee and sat by the table again.

"Sure. This isn't the first time. I'm screwed for a long time, from the insurance company and my job." I took a deep breath. "I'm so alone. I don't feel like anyone likes me. No one loves me."

"We all do, honey," Nancy said. She got up and enveloped me within the folds of her arms. "I'm so sorry life has been full of sticks and stones for you, but we've always loved you."

"Thank you," I said. Sniffling, I clung to Nancy. "We all need each other."

"Let it all out, sweetie," Nancy said. "You're with someone who loves you."

"Mike dropping you like that cheated you out of your life. Sharon should've seen how you were hurting and told you more about him. She wouldn't have had to say much, just a little to help you feel better about yourself."

"Thank you. I've always wondered and felt like I

had something wrong with me. Like he saw me, scrunched up his nose like I stunk, then broke it off. I thought I either smelled like a rotten fish or looked like one. I dearly, deeply loved Mike." Nancy frowned. "Paul treated me like a princess. It's my fault the marriage didn't last. If only I'd known then what I know now about myself, about life."

"At least now you do know that you were the love of his life. He did love you. You didn't stink. You were beautiful. You couldn't see that you were lovable because of the breakup. That's why you couldn't let Paul into your heart. You were afraid of being dumped in an instant, just like what had happened. You were scared of a repeat."

"I never thought of my marriage in that way, but you're right. I probably was scared Paul would drop me like a hot potato," Nancy said. "I feel as if a dark cloud hanging over me has finally evaporated. Thank you, Judy. Thank you for this weekend and for forcing us to see ourselves for who we are."

"What are friends for? You're welcome. As for me? I'm going to get myself clean and sober and enjoy myself from here on out."

"Thank God! It's time for us to get to know each other and enjoy one another."

"For whatever time we have left."

"Well, I don't want to talk about 'time left.' It's time for me to clean up," Nancy said. She began returning refrigerated items into the refrigerator and stacking the remaining dirty dishes. "Don't worry about a thing, Judy. You do what you need to while I take care of the kitchen mess."

"Thank you," I said.

I went out to the living room to make a private phone call to my department chair. This was one phone conversation I wasn't looking forward to.

Nancy
Chapter Eight

The skies were still overcast and I worried how the next few days with Judy would go. I'll try hard to not be a smother-mother as she wouldn't appreciate it. Judy's health was also a concern but having her with me for a few days will bring us both physical and mental healing.

As I finished wiping around the stove, table, and other needed places, Judy reentered the kitchen.

"What's the verdict?"

"I'm waiting to hear from the police so I can pick up my belongings."

"That might be a wait?"

"It's hard to say but I'm happy for Sharon's clothes. My suitcase only had the one dress and shoes. I planned to slip into the outfit I'd worn for the trip. It was clean," Judy said. "I've sent messages, one to my department chair at work, the other to my insurance agent. I'm also waiting for Carl to phone." She smiled at me. "I do feel better today."

"Good. Tell me about Carl? You two still friends?"

"Yes. I'm not sure what I would do without him. He never remarried and we speak frequently," Judy said. Her phone rang, and she answered. "Carl, thank you for calling."

Since she was still talking, I went upstairs to get ready for the day. I hadn't showered the night before, so now was my chance. A half-hour later, I was dressed in a pair of jeans, white blouse, and black blazer. I put on red earrings to match my lipstick. I wore little makeup, foundation and mascara. I met Judy in the kitchen, still in her bathrobe.

"How is Carl?" I asked.

"Great! He'll book a Thursday morning flight on his card and pick me up at the airport," Judy said. Her phone dinged a few times, indicating she'd received messages. "My boss texted me and told me a student worker will take over the class until I return. I can email lesson plans. The worker already knows German, so it shouldn't be a problem. Not like high school where the subs usually don't speak the language." She thought a moment. "I might retire."

"I think that sounds good. We can see each other more often."

"True. I'd like that," Judy said. She read through the rest of her messages. "The agent gave me the go ahead to have the car totaled." Judy waited a beat and said, "I can now get my things from the car."

"This all is good news. I'll take you to the car before we go to my house," I said. "Sharon's clothes fit you nicely."

"They feel great. I'm all stiff and sore so I'm happy about the fit. I appreciate what you're doing, Nancy. You're a good friend."

"Oh gosh! We're in this together. You'd do the same for me." I glanced around the room. "I think it's cleaned to Sharon's satisfaction. Let's get her clothes in a bag and you bundled up."

"I'll start, but I have a request. I want a *Starbucks.*"

"There's one not too far away," I called after Judy while she climbed the stairs to place Sharon's clothes inside a bag to bring down.

"I haven't had a chance to really ramble around the house," Judy said. She was coming back down the stairs. "There are so many old things, antiques, such as the furniture and cabinet china that remind me of my growing up years. Most of these items must've been inherited." An album lay on the bottom bookshelf so she sat with it. "Look at this album, Nancy. It's wonderful."

"Let me see," I said. I sat down beside Judy.

The small, four-by-four pictures before me brought back memories. Sharon filled the beginning pages with images of her family. All of her siblings. There was Sharon, Jill, Kaye, Mike, Peter, and their parents. Tears filled my eyes once again as I remembered meeting them all. It was as clear as a bell. I wished for more time.

"All set?"

"You bet." I set the album aside. "Let's go."

With my suitcase in hand, and Judy with her bag, we headed out to my car, locking the door behind us.

"I hope Sharon won't be too busy while I'm here," Judy said.

"Me, too." Opening the trunk, we placed our things inside before closing the lid. We walked toward the doors and both climbed inside, buckling up in unison.

"I hope this person Sharon is hooked up with is good to her." I looked out the sideview mirror for approaching cars. "After we get home and you settled in, I'm going to search for my teenage diaries."

"You really have kept them?" Judy asked.

"Yes. There's a reason and purpose for everything. I wonder if the diaries hold the missing key to Vicky's disappearance?" I said. I drove onto the street and headed toward the impound lot where we got Judy's luggage.

"They might. We can always hope the police will be able to pick up on some little tidbit of info from your chicken scratches," Judy said.

"Yes, exactly. A little bit of knowledge from something I'd written down."

We drove through the nearby coffee house drive-thru for our drinks before entry onto the main highway. My house wasn't more than an hour drive from Sharon's, but the scenery was illustrious. The sky had opened and the sun shone through, exposing the brilliant silver and orange leaves of the maple trees.

"What do you think happened to her?" I asked.

"It's hard to say. She could've been *beamed* in a *nano second,* as Robin Williams said or William Shatner in those old TV shows. Your guess is as good as mine."

"One thing we didn't think about, is that she could easily be alive," I said.

"True. Wouldn't she have wanted to contact her parents or return home by now?"

"What if she couldn't return or wanted to spare

them the heartache of what happened to her? Like rape or sold into slavery?" I tried to imagine what I would've done under those circumstances.

"We're speculating."

"Is it possible that she's right under our nose?"

Judy
Chapter Nine

We were silent the rest of the way to her house, both deep in thought. Vicky was certainly on my mind and I'd venture to say she was on Nancy's. Where on earth was she? She could be anywhere. Prom night went beautifully. We all danced and paraded around like princesses, except Nancy, who didn't attend because of her Mike. I hope that soon Sharon will reveal everything to her surrounding his death so she can get on with her life and find happiness. Go for trips and enjoy herself—maybe remarry. That would be a trip!

"Here we are," Nancy said, turning into her driveway.

"Nice digs." The brick front and side screened-in porch were cute and comfy looking. I was sure that the interior was the same. I unbuckled once we'd entered the garage and the door went down. I swung my legs out of the car but couldn't stand. "Help me up. I think my legs are stuck."

"Yep." Nancy scooted over and helped pull me up to standing. "I think the ride stiffened you up."

"You're not alone in that thought," I said. I admonished myself for the sarcasm. I needed to be more contrite. I hadn't been nice for a very long time. *Was it depression based?*

"Let's get you inside," Nancy said. "I'll walk you to the living room where you can sit comfortably while I go back for the suitcases."

While I stood in the middle of her living room, I stared out of the front window. It was a beautiful view of trees and squirrels. The squirrels chased each other up and down tree trunks. Watching them amused me until Nancy returned.

"It gorgeous here. Is this where you lived with Paul?"

"Yes. He left one day and never returned. I got papers in the mail and signed them. He was justified and very truthful. The declaration stated that I'd get the house and car, he'd get what little there was in the savings plus his truck. That's all there was to it," Nancy said. "Just like that!" She snapped her fingers. "I've always loved it here and so I stayed. The neighbors come and go. It's not like it used to be where we all knew each other and grew up together."

"The question is, did we really know each other? Who really does?"

"That's true. Look at us. What secrets have we kept locked in our hearts to reveal fifty years later?" Nancy said.

"We can live side-by-side, walk to school together everyday for thirteen years but not know each other. We all hold truths that aren't to be told. We have wishes and wants that are dear to us that aren't expressed. We have inner thoughts, which no one hears. Maybe we're with people who don't want to hear. That makes us alone."

"And lonely."

"Then we have Sharon. She was born just the way she is. It's not a learned behavior, we both know that. Think of how lonely she is," I said.

"We'll invite her and her friend over before you leave," Nancy said. "We need to offer her as much support as possible." Nancy reached for my coat and hung it in the closet. "Have a seat or take a look around. Snoop as much as you want."

"I presume my room is at the end of the hallway?"

"On the left, across from mine. The bathroom's right beside it. Make yourself comfortable. I'm going to strip into some cozy clothes."

Nancy carried my suitcase into the room as I followed.

"Where are the albums?" I asked.

"They're in my suitcase, it's stuffed."

I watched as Nancy went into her room before going into mine. I hung my and Sharon's clothes in the closet.

The bed was a little stiffer than preferred, but I figured it wouldn't prevent me from a good night sleep. The pillow was light and fluffy. A few minutes of alone time gave me a chance to think about my department chair, Magdalene the Great. She'd warned me about my drinking and had ordered me once to seek treatment, which, of course, I didn't do. I was pretty sure she'd have her way this time around. I wasn't looking forward to it. It was also going to be tough to refrain from alcohol while staying with Nancy. I worried that our friendship would end if I opened the flask secreted in my suitcase.

Be brave.

I dug to the bottom of the suitcase where it was hidden and removed the flask. No more temptations, I told myself, and tucked it into a pocket and headed to the bathroom. Once inside, I emptied it in the sink and ran a lot of hot water. My hands shook, but knowing it was for the betterment of us both, I tried to relax with a few deep breaths.

After finishing my business, I went back to my room where I returned the flask.

As I was ready to walk down the hallway to the living room, my phone rang. It was Sharon.

"Hi hon," Sharon said. "I'm sorry it worked out this way, but it couldn't be helped."

"You need a job with decent hours, girlfriend, this is ridiculous! Do you ever sleep?"

"That's a good question." I could almost hear her grinning. "How are the clothes?"

"They're behaving and not giving me a squeegee in places they don't belong, so good. I thank you for them. Really I do."

"That's good to know, and maybe more than I need to know," Sharon said. "I'm going to begin to search tomorrow in our church records for names and dates of individuals who may have been patients at the old Soldiers' Home. I'll keep you both informed."

"We were talking about you anyway. Why don't I let you speak to Nancy?" I began walking over to Nancy's bedroom where she was found.

"Sure."

"It's about coming out one night," I said. I handed Nancy the phone.

Since I was hearing one side of the conversation, I took the albums and continued to the living room.

The couch looked inviting so I plopped down on it. I opened Nancy's album, and the back photo was of her Mike in his dress blue Marines uniform. He was so handsome and his eyes were the bluest eyes I'd ever seen. I'd also have liked to know the secret of his death. Being found frozen outside the veteran's facility, begged questions. I hoped all of Nancy's questions would soon be answered.

I continued glancing through the pictures, stopping to study certain ones. The pictures of us three before graduation were the most revealing because we looked so happy. You could almost see our future in our bright eyes and beautiful smiles.

Nancy sat beside me and we continued studying the photo pages. She placed my phone on the coffee table.

"Stop right there," Nancy said. "Where is this one taken?"

"It must be by Minnehaha Falls," I said.

"Let's put that one aside. See?" Nancy said. "There's some movement in the background. There are shadows near the flowers. And someone watching us over in the corner near the depot. See it?"

"I sure do. It's like you two were being watched." I removed it, setting it aside. "It's almost spooky. What did Sharon say?"

"She'll come for dinner one night before you leave.

That will give her time to search records and for her girlfriend to line up a babysitter."

"Good! What will we serve? Let me pay for it," I said.

"I'll check the freezer in the morning to see what we have around here to eat."

"Groceries tomorrow and now back to the photos."

There were several albums to keep us busy for the day. As we worked our way through them, Nancy made sandwiches for lunch and later we ordered a pizza for supper. Neither of us felt like cooking.

"We have gobs of us at birthday parties but quit taking pictures as we got older. No selfies," I said. "It's too bad that technology wasn't up to nowadays standards." I picked up a photo from the pile. "I think this might be another of Vicky's old boyfriends. She had a ton. Always dating."

"Yeah, and so did Margo. You too. I was always jealous because my soldier boy was off fighting the war," Nancy said. "I wonder if he suffered from Post Traumatic Stress Syndrome? You know, PTSD?" She looked at me, flushed. "I bet he did. The poor guy."

"You're probably right with that one since he was found dead in front of a veterans facility." I yawned so hard, I thought my jaw would crack. "I'm really ready for the sack." *As well as a nightcap. Is there still a drop in the flask?"*

I said, "Good night," and went to the bedroom, closing the door behind me. I dug out the flask and tipped it backward. Not a drop of whiskey left. *How could I have been so stupid as to dump it down the drain?*

I was flipping back the covers when Nancy knocked on the door.

"Sleep well, Judy. If you're in want or need of anything, like an aspirin, let me know or else you'll find it in the bathroom cabinet."

"Thanks, Nancy, I'm sorry I cut out so fast but the sleepies hit like a thunderbolt."

"No problem. Good night."

"You too."

She was darn sweet, I told myself. She would've made for a wonderful mother. Patient and kind came to mind when I thought of her.

My fingers were shaky as I plugged my phone in for recharging. It'd been forty-eight hours since my last alcoholic drink. My stomach lurched a little, too. I debated the wisdom of sending Carl a message because of the time. He went to bed early and it was already ten o'clock. I did anyway. *I'm in bed. When I got to Nancy's, I poured my liquor down the drain. I'm shaking. I need a drink.* I sent the message.

Barely were my eyes closed when the phone dinged a response. It read: *Rinse your face with warm water, or take a shower. Stand up and stretch. Find a book or think about your favorite meal. Try not to take an aspirin, if you don't need it for pain. Keep me informed, Judy, I insist. You're doing the right thing. C*

I sent him a heart emoji. He responded with: *send an emoji every time you're awake. Let me know how you feel.*

A thumbs-up emoji was sent.

I crawled farther down into the blankets, shut my eyes and fell right asleep. Two hours later, I used the facility and woke from that time on every hour but didn't send him an emoji every time. He didn't need to know how restless I slept.

Nancy
Chapter Ten

The diary lay open across my chest when I woke to use the restroom during the night. I made a dog-ear on the page before setting it aside on my bed stand. The morning brought a cloudless sky. With the two diaries in hand, I walked out to the kitchen. I loved sitting and enjoying the view outside but today would be different. It was already near nine, and usually, I was up a few hours earlier.

Coffee smelled wonderful from the automatic brew pot, and I poured myself a cup. As I sipped from the cup, I reread certain passages that had piqued my interest the night before. I grabbed a notepad and began jotting down information that might be relevant in a new search for Vicky. I glanced up as Judy entered.

"Pour yourself a cup and relax," I said. Judy looked pale and weak. "You look like you didn't sleep. Is everything all right?"

"I'm fine," Judy said. She ran her fingers through her hair. "I didn't sleep the best. I'm sure an afternoon nap will take care of it."

"I suppose different bed and pillows," I said. "I have some things to show you. I want to know what you think."

"I'm not sure if I can think straight or not," Judy said. "I propose that we eat a bowl of cereal or toast and go for a drive to Minnehaha Falls. I'd like to walk around and go to where the old Soldier's Home used to be."

"We can do that. Then we'll have a better picture in our mind," I said. I set the diaries aside. "There are a few pages where I made notes, then jotted them onto the pad. Take a look."

Spring 1970

1. *That man was there again. I hate him. He stared at me when we went to see Vicky's dad. I wonder who he is?*

2. *Vicky told me she hates him and won't go again to see her dad unless she must.*

"Do you think it's the same man we saw in the picture near the depot?"

"It could be. We should make a note of it and the picture," Judy said.

"You're right." I penciled a few relevant words beside the entry with today's date on it.

"I wonder if her dad knew about that guy?" Judy said. She got up and made herself a slice of toast. "This is a perfect breakfast. I never eat much."

"Mr. Storbaekkene has been deceased for several years, I think." I poured myself a bowl of Cheerios and sat down once again by the table. "There are a few other references to that man. I don't recall ever learning his name."

"They must've been making-out down near the Home. I used to and was chased out a few times," Judy said. She buttered her toast and began to eat it. "More coffee? Gasoline, as my dad used to call it." She filled both of our cups. "I wonder if Sharon would be able to figure out his name?"

"I think we need to speak to Diane. She should know the name of that guy and maybe a little more for us to go on," Nancy said. "Let's finish up here and then take off."

We took turns in the bathroom and when I returned to the kitchen, Judy was on her phone speaking to someone. I hated to eavesdrop, but it couldn't be helped.

"I called Carl so he knows what I'm doing," Judy said. "He's been worried about me and my state of mind. He's always looked after me. My guardian angel."

"I think you've needed about ten of those," I said. "I'm glad you're still good friends." I hesitated then said, "In the spirit of no secrets, what's with you two?"

"I'm not sure. He says he still loves me and he's never remarried. I don't understand it myself. However, I'm not so sure I could marry anyone else because I still love him."

"What happened with you two?" I handed Judy her coat and reached for mine. "If you both love each other?"

"Marijuana and alcohol got in the way. It's my fault, really." Judy zipped her coat and said, "Ready for Minnesota!"

"Good luck with that! No one is ever ready for the weather around here." I wrapped a scarf around my neck and grabbed my purse that had the car keys inside of it. "All set."

"Let's get a *Starbucks,*" Judy said.

"Already on my radar."

We climbed into the car, buckling up. Soon, I backed out of the garage and closed the overhead door behind me. It felt good to have Judy once more beside me as we tootled down the road again.

"I wonder if the kids still drag-race up and down Lake Street?" Judy said.

"I doubt it. The cops are always out patrolling. That area has changed so much, it's unbelievable." I turned into the drive-thru of the nearest coffee shop and ordered two medium sized lattes. "Here," I said, handing one to her. We drove away and headed toward south Minneapolis.

"The trees lining the Minnesota River are gorgeous. This is where the Sioux Indians camped and traded goods with the white man. It once belonged to them," Judy said. "It's really sad isn't it, when you see the pollution and what we've done to the water supply?"

"At least we have good people helping to clean the rivers and streams," I said. "There's hope. Now, the invasive species are killing our native fish." I shook my head. "It's too depressing. I don't want to talk about it."

"Pigs Eye is right over there, where our first state capitol used to be. Fort Snelling right there, too, by the airport plus the cemetery of Fort Snelling for our vets. It's so gorgeous around here. The Mall of America off to our left."

"We'll have to find time to stop in there," I said, following Highway 13 to the bridge. "I miss seeing the Ford Plant. I suspect, so do the former employees."

"Well, we're almost there. Let's make a detour and drive past Howe, Sanford, and good old Roosevelt."

"Sure."

I turned onto River Road before making a turn on 38th St. and passed our grade school.

"Flowers in the front, a small garden in the back, and the building looks like new. Now Sanford," Judy said.

I turned onto 42nd Avenue that brought us past our junior high school, Sanford.

"It's been added onto and looks just as nice and new as before." I remembered being filmed by the librarian as we entered the main door on our first day of school. "Do you remember the first day of school and being filmed?"

"I remember it but don't remember seeing it. What about those paper days? They were fun, we could wear pants. We collected all those newspapers and tied them up. Each classroom had a marked area on the boulevard."

"Recycling," I said. "Now for Roosevelt."

"Does Vicky's mom still live across from the park?"

"Yes. She probably never wanted to move in case Vicky should miraculously return," I said.

I turned the corner and headed up to our old high school.

"Do you think if we walked around inside, it

would help with our memory of Vicky?" Judy asked.

"It's hard to say, but all we need to focus on is prom night," I said.

We slowly drove past it. In its heyday, we had one way hallways because of the large student population.

"So many memories. Plays, hockey games, pep fests. When I took shorthand, I dictated once in class because I wanted to see if that teacher of ours could do it too. She drove me crazy. Typing and shorthand. However, I'm thankful for typing because of learning the keyboard and how to type form letters."

"Me too," Judy said.

"This is enjoyable." I started toward Minnehaha Falls. "Should we park by the falls? I think it's for the best."

"Yes, then we can walk around," Judy said. "Old times and sweet memories."

I saw her hand shake when she grabbed her coffee.

"It hit the spot," I said.

"Yes."

I wondered what was going through Judy's mind. I knew she'd been a drinker and there'd been an allusion to a missing toke in her purse. I glanced at her.

"I'm fine, Nancy. Quit looking at me." Judy eyed me. "Let's walk. The fresh air will be good for us both."

We paid the parking fee with a credit card and began our journey up to the palladium where there was a restaurant. The menu was basically seafood, but it all sounded good.

"Let's grab a bite."

"Agreed."

"It's still just as beautiful here as it ever was."

"It is, but a bit chilly to sit outside."

We ordered grilled mahi mahi and steamed shrimp and went to find a table for ourselves. As we ate, we watched the people stroll nearby. When finished, we walked around the park. The mushy ground was cumbersome in places, but we circled the waterfall, taking the cobbled steps down and around that brought us back up. The falls was magnificent and I wished for my camera but used my phone instead.

Our next area to explore was near the John H. Stevens House, and the birthplace of the name of 'Minneapolis,' and the government structure for Hennepin County. The Princess Depot sat nearby. It was called "Princess" because of its delicate gingerbread canopy.

We circled these two structures and kept walking along the flower gardens trail toward our destination.

The Home didn't look the same because of the upgrades over the years. It'd been built in 1887 for the Civil War veterans. Cottages were made for the men to stay in and one for women. Now, it was part of veteran's homes across the country.

"Do you think the person who abducted her was a Civil War soldier?" I asked. We'd stopped near it and sat on a nearby bench seat. "There's also Korea."

"The Civil War soldiers would've been dead," Judy said. "It could've been someone from either the second world war or Korea."

"True," I said. "Let's just sit here for a while. We

have a magnificent view of the area. Let's try to remember what it was like down here in 1970."

"Good thought," Judy said. "Let's make individual notes on our phones. There's a bench over on the far side. I'm going to sit over there. It'll give me a different point of view than yours."

"That's a great idea."

I stayed where I was and closed my eyes. An impression of Vicky came to mind. I pictured her in ponytails and her bright smile. I remembered playing hopscotch with her and jumprope. I tried to envision her the night of the prom. Unfortunately, I lost focus from a nearby honking horn. I opened my eyes and studied the ground before me. What had changed besides the entryway? New growth surrounding the new section of the hospital was easily identified. I could picture me and Mike down here, parking and steaming up the windows. Judy and her boyfriends. Vicky and Margo, too. Everyone came down here to park or else in the lot near the waterfall, which didn't exist anymore. It was called, "the deer pen."

I glanced over to where Judy should be sitting, but she'd moved away, and I decided to walk around, too.

Judy
Chapter Eleven

The old growth of oak and maple trees was stunning for this time of the year. Course, it always was. Minnesota was known for its beautiful parks and waterways, but this was special. I'd decided to poke around to try and get a feel of the land and the way it once had been—way back when—so many years ago. Walking around down in this little hollow wouldn't have been my taste as a kid nor, I dare say, for any of my friends during the growing up years. I did remember my parents mentioning in passing about "going-ons" at the Soldier's Home and to stay away, that the patients were mentally ill. PTSD dated back to the beginning of time, I reckoned.

I continued walking around the trees and the undergrowth, heading toward the sound of the rushing water. The ground was bumpy and the footing terrible, causing me to trip and fall.

"Ouch!" I grumbled, landing right on my rear end. *Just what I needed. How am I going to explain this one? Or get up?* Besides the horrible car accident, I hadn't had any harm done to me in many years. I'm not sure how long it'd been since I sat on the floor and tried to get up! Slowly, but surely, I raised myself up to my knees and then tried to put my butt in the air and hopefully raise upward. It didn't work. I crawled on my hands and knees to the nearest large tree. Fortunately, it wasn't that far away. With one hand over the other, I tried climbing my way up to standing. At last, I was up on my own two feet. Hallelujah! And pass the beans! Next on the agenda after brushing myself off to the best of my ability, I searched for my phone and found it on the ground but not broken. Just dirty. *There is a God.*

I debated sending a message to Nancy and telling her about it but decided to wait. She'd find out soon enough. That woman had eyes in the back of her head and a nose for anything that didn't relate to her, and she should've been called Nancy Snoopy at times.

Since there was nothing coincidental in my book, I gave the area a good scrutiny. There was a rock embedded in the ground that reminded me of an old tombstone and the ground in front of it was depressed. The features raised my curiosity. I sent Nancy a message:

I'm in the east woods and located something odd.

Okay. I'll look for you.

I knew she'd find me. I hadn't brought my scarf or anything at all that could be used as a marker so I hated to leave the spot for fear of not finding it again. While Nancy searched for me, I studied the surrounding area for possible other similar stones. At the same time, Nancy sent me a message:

I found a stone that looks like a cemetery marker. Is that what you found?

Yes, but I don't have a means to mark it so we can easily

find it.

I can on mine with a scarf. I'll tie it around a nearby tree. I'll be right there.

Ok

Off in the distance, I studied the undergrowth for signs of more indicators or land depressions. I wondered if Nancy's spotting was depressed? What caused the sunken-in land? A removed large tree stump? An oak tree may have been removed. Or was a body buried under all the weeds?

Nancy appeared at the same time as a park ranger.

"I received a message that a woman was standing alone in the nearby woods. That she might need help and you must be her. Then another message appeared that stated there were two women in the woods but where is the second?" the ranger said. "My name is Rick."

"Rick the Ranger, it has a nice ring. The second is in back of you," I said. "I'm Judy and she's Nancy. It's funny that you should materialize at just this time."

"Nancy?" Rick turned and saw Nancy approaching.

"In the flesh," Nancy said. "Hi. Why are you here?"

"He's checking up on us old buddies. Now, Rick the Ranger, here's the scoop." I reached over and touched the curious stone and said, "Why is this here? Look at the depression it has made, which we're actually standing in. It's different from the rest of ground. Can't you see it?"

"Let's step back," Rick said.

We moved several steps farther away and stood with our arms folded across our fronts and stared at the area, just like the Three Stooges—Larry, Moe, and Curly.

"What do you think?" I said. "Doesn't it look like someone was buried?"

"And its depressed because there isn't a coffin," Nancy said.

"Curious," Rick said. He massaged his chin. "Ladies, you've moved my day from humdrum to mysterious. How about if I go and speak to my boss about this? See what he has to say." He glanced from me to Nancy.

"Before you leave us," Nancy said, "I have one to show you. It's over there." She nodded in the direction.

"Lead onward," I said.

We followed Nancy's lead and located the scarf. The three of us stood over the stone until Rick broke the silence.

"Weird."

"Not only weird, but strange," I said. "You'd think I was seeing double or on dope."

"Shush now, Judy, he'll think we're dope heads!"

"You two? Never. However, I do wonder about a few of your bruises," Rick said, looking at me.

"Car accident. I promise. Nothing other than that."

"Let me take down your names and numbers," Rick said. He reached into his pocket and removed two of his cards and handed them to each of us. "In case you see any more." He jotted down our cell numbers.

"I live in Madison now," I said to explain my area code.

"Got them down."

"We neglected to tell you the real reason we're here," Nancy said.

"Let me tell him," I said. "You're stealing my thunder."

"I'm waiting," Rick said. He looked at me.

I took a deep breath. I hadn't realized how much anger, hurt, and love was mixed up inside of me until this very moment. I wiped my eyes and blew my nose.

"It's like this. You see, Nancy and myself plus two other women had been friends since childhood. A friend, Margo, was just buried two days ago. The mother and brother of another friend visited us later, after the funeral."

"I see. And what does this have to do with anything?"

"The fourth was abducted the night of our senior prom and has never been found. Vicky Storbaekkene. When we spoke with Vicky's mom and brother Will, we realized that maybe we can help with the investigation."

"What year are we talking about?"

"Roosevelt, 1970."

"Cold case," Nancy said. "She was last seen with her boyfriend here, making out, after prom. We all came down here to make-out. It's not done anymore mostly because of security, I suppose."

"Interesting. What else do you know?"

"Not much except that her dad worked here and there was a patient that bothered her and he bothered me too whenever I'd come along," Nancy said. "I don't know the patient's name."

"Now my day has shifted to interesting." Rick took a breath and stared at us. "Tell you what? I'll tell my superior everything you've told me, and we'll let the wheels spin from there."

"Sounds like a plan," I said. "Thank you. He should be able to tell you why the depression is there. It could be from a stump removal."

"Right," Rick said. "Now let me escort you two ladies to the Stevens House where you can continue onto the waterfall area."

"Sure," Nancy said.

The three of us trudged across the ground to flatter trails until at last arriving at the house.

"Thanks," I said again, "and please look into it right away."

"I will."

When we were out of ear range, I said, "I'm hungry again and we need to talk."

"Not before you tell me why you look like you've been squirrel hunting."

"I knew it! You're like a blood hound, I swear, it's in your DNA." *I can't get away with anything while she's around.* "I tripped and fell and had to crawl on my hands and knees to a tree and then climb up it in order to stand. There! Are you happy!"

"Oh my!" Nancy chuckled. "This is one for the record books. I'm telling Sharon."

"Go right ahead. Everyone needs a laugh," I said. It didn't take long before a grin covered my face.

"Let's go some place and have a cup of coffee or a piece of pie."

"Sounds good."

It didn't take long before we had jumped into the car, and Nancy was driving toward the nearest neighborhood diner. There was a corner one near the church. She easily found a spot to park and we went inside.

The smell inside made my tummy flip-flop from hunger and my mouth water. Chicken soup and dumplings. I could pick out the odor from a mile away. That and homemade apple pie. We took a window seat and quietly gazed out the window.

"This is a nice, quiet neighborhood," Nancy said. "It's just like when we grew up. It's almost as if time stood still."

"I love it here. I'm glad you thought of this place."

The waitress came and we placed identical orders, apple pie a la mode and coffee.

"What do you think is going to happen?" Nancy asked.

"No idea. Not a clue." I shut my mouth and stared out the window, watching an old woman walk down the street. "Before the student lunch program kicked in, we used to go home and eat lunch. You went to your grandparents, and the neighbor lady came to our house since my mom worked. Diane used to go into the homes and make meals and watch the kids when they'd come home for lunch break, didn't she? So where would Vicky have gone for lunch if her mom wasn't home? She may have gone to be with her dad for that time, but he would've been at work. However, their neighbor lady, Mrs. Eidsmoe, used to have us come for a cookie or else we'd pester her in the summer when she was out weeding the flowerbeds. I bet she made lunch for Vicky and Will."

"It's all speculation, but I bet you're right that Mrs. Eidsmoe made their lunches. Why?" She looked out the window also. "Where is this going?"

"I'm not sure. I wonder if the police are aware of this?"

"I'm sure, but we're talking about high school and by that time, we were eating in school or leaving campus and going to a drive-thru if we were lucky enough to have a car."

The waitress returned with our pie and coffee.

"Thanks," we said in unison.

"That's all true, but do you think any of the people Diane took care of would have something to do with Vicky's abduction?" I asked.

"I have my doubts. That was a long time before we became teenagers," Nancy said. "What makes you think that?"

"I'm not sure. Do you remember who Mr. and Mrs. Storbaekkene hung around with? Family picnics? My parents used to have card parties once in a while. Mom would invite the neighbors. Who were the Storbaekkene's neighbors? Any idea?" I said.

"That's a good question. We need to ask Diane. Will might remember a few things too, like the man from the Home or recognize the man near the depot."

"I'd like to ask Will if he knew of any of his friends that may have been interested in Vicky or if he could remember anything out of the ordinary happening when she'd go and babysit."

"Now that's a thought, too," Nancy said. "These are good questions to make note of."

I took a pen and old receipt from my purse and jotted down the questions so as not to forget them.

"This is what I have: Neighbor names. Man at the Home and depot picture man. Friends of Will's interested in her. Who Diane made lunches for. Card parties. Can you think of anything else to ask?"

"Not at the moment," Nancy said.

We finished our meal, paid our bill, and went out to the car.

"Let's drive past our old houses on the way home," Nancy said.

"Fine by me." I settled back and watched the world go by. I'd forgotten to send Carl a message so I took care of it. I knew I was blessed to have him still in my life.

It was a wonderful drive, a lovely day. It did feel good to be back at Nancy's.

When we'd hung up our coats and collapsed on the living room furniture, I called Sharon.

"I'm glad that you called." I could almost picture Sharon sipping a cup of coffee with us.

"What news do you have?" I asked.

"I have a few names from the church records that might be of interest. Also, I have an appointment for tomorrow morning at the Soldiers' Home.

"Tell me about the church records," I said.

"Vicky's boyfriend's parents, the Turners, are listed as deceased."

"We went to Minnehaha Falls today."

"What did you find? Anything interesting?"

"Besides Ranger Rick, this is what we both happened upon or should I say, I fell upon and Nancy happened upon?" I went ahead and told her the story of our morning ending with our phone call promise for tomorrow on or around the same time to compare notes.

I clicked from the phone and turned to Nancy to tell her Sharon's report.

"Where do you think today and Rick will lead?" I asked.

"Hopefully, to another lead."

"I want a good discovery not just a lead. Something with substance."

Nancy
Chapter Twelve

We spent the rest of the afternoon resting. We had a light supper and both of us showered right afterward. I inserted into the DVD player the movie, *American Graffiti,* popped a large bowl of popcorn, and we enjoyed ourselves.

"I've had fun." I looked at Judy as the final credits rolled across the screen. "We need to be together more often. Have you considered moving to Minneapolis? The weather isn't that much different."

"Right now, I can't think of it. I have to make things right with the university. My department chair isn't too happy with yours truly."

"And, Carl? You? Will you retire?"

"I'm contracted for this school year. Who knows? They might revoke my contract and just let me go. Either way, I'm going in for treatment. I want to like myself."

"What do you mean by that remark?"

"I'm tired of drinking. I'm tired of being stoned and still teaching. The kids deserved a better teacher. Shame on me. I want a relationship with someone and I hope it's Carl. Since I haven't had a drink, I'm feeling better. Last night, I felt like I'd explode without one, but that's past. In my mind, I know I must do this."

"There are AA meetings all over town," I said. "It'll be good for you to be around friends who love you, no matter how goofy you are." I grinned. "Seriously though, move back here."

"I'll give it some thought." Judy stood and picked up the dishes. "I'm pooped and need to hit the sack."

"Yes, it's been a long day." I got up to remove the DVD from the player. "I'm going to stay up for a little bit and skim my diaries once more."

"All right. Good night."

I turned the TV station to the news, grabbed the diaries, and started to read further in the pages. I wanted to see if there was anything written about Steve. If I liked him or not. If he'd worn something cool or dorky. Just what I thought of him or if there were secrets from either Judy, Vicky, Margo, or Sharon.

My mind drifted to Mike as I read my entrants.

Mike softly kissed my neck when I laid my head on his shoulder. We were dancing slow. I felt like I'd died and gone to heaven. I kept stepping on his toes. Our knees kept knocking together. His hands on my back felt wonderful. I wanted more.

"Mike, what happened?" I whispered.

I looked at the news segment but had trouble focusing. My mind was stuck on Mike. I wished Sharon had given me a little more information concerning his health and well-being at the time of his death. I wondered if she was awake and decided to give her a call.

"Sharon?"

"Nancy?"

"I need to know. I can't think straight. My mind is on Mike, and it's hard to think about finding Vicky and hunting down leads of her whereabouts. Please give me information about him. Please?"

"Nancy. He was my favorite brother. I miss him dearly."

"I know you do, but I can't continue living like this," I said. I sighed, brushing the hair from my eyes. "I hate not knowing anything about his death."

"He had PTSD, big time," Sharon said. "You know what that is, don't you?"

"Yes, of course. I figured that was part of his illness."

"You don't know half of it," Sharon said. "Agent Orange ate his insides and also his brain. He couldn't think very well. It caused medical issues galore. He just plain wasn't himself from the moment he returned home from his first tour of duty in Vietnam."

"Finally. Finally you tell me what happened to him. After all of these years." Tears filled my eyes. "That poor man. My heart breaks even more for him. For us."

"When Judy returns home, we'll get together and I'll explain it all to you."

"Can't you tell me why he was found frozen outside of the veterans facility?"

"He was seeking treatment but was constantly turned away. I'm sure he thought if he could just get there early."

"My poor Mike." Tears streamed down my cheeks.

"I'm saying 'good night,' Nancy. I have tears in my eyes too. We need to be together and alone when Mike's discussed."

"You're right. I can see that now. I'm sorry for bothering you. Good night."

Teary eyed, I went to bed.

Sharon was the dearest person in the world. I would've been happy to have her as a sister-in-law. It was too bad the stars weren't aligned for it to happen. I knew she was close to Mike. He knew me inside out and upside down. Paul never did. If I said, "Yes," he'd respond, "No." If I thought going to a movie sounded like fun, he'd say, "No, we're going to an antique car show." I'd plant flowers around the house, he'd dig them up and plant strawberries. I'd developed a negative taste for them. I hated them.

I placed the diary on the bed stand and shut off the light. Upon closing my eyes, I tried to erase Mike from my thoughts, but he never faded.

Was it first love – last love?

Somehow, I managed a decent night worth of sleep. I only woke twice to use the facility, and I never heard Judy during the night. It was amazing. I rolled over and flipped the blankets off and sat on the bed side. I was one step closer to discovering what had happened to Mike, after all of these years! It made me feel lighter. If only someone would've opened up to me years ago, then maybe my marriage would've worked.

I knew there was more news to come.

After yawning and stretching a little bit, I drifted

to the bathroom and started my morning chores. I heard the coffee pot perking and the clattering of dishes and figured Judy was after her first cup of coffee for the day.

I strolled to the kitchen and found her sitting with a roll in hand and the other holding a coffee cup.

"I'm going after the newspaper," I said. I walked to the front door, found the newspaper on the doorstep, and brought it back to the kitchen.

"I'll pour you a cup."

"Brr, it's chilly." I plunked into my chair and opened the paper. "I called Sharon last night. I probably shouldn't have because of upsetting her. Losing Mike was terrible for her, and it was about the same time that her mother died."

"What did she tell you?" Judy sipped her coffee and looked at me over the cup rim.

"About the PTSD and Agent Orange, how it affected his body and brain. It helps. I didn't know how bad it was for him. That makes sense for being found outside of the veterans facility. He'd been turned down many times and thought if he could get in right away to see a doctor…but, of course, it wasn't meant to happen."

"Nancy. You dear sweet woman. I feel so bad for you. Next time, she'll tell you more, I bet."

"It helped." Images of Mike floated through my thoughts. Mike, smiling from ear to ear. His baby blue eyes lit up the room and so did his smile. He couldn't keep his hands off me, nor could I from him. In the beginning Sharon chaperoned when we went to a n movie. Later, he'd told me it was because I wa... ny and quiet, that I'd feel better. I remember turning red as a beet, I knew we were more than boyfriend/girlfriend friendship.

We were destined for each other.

I went to the toaster and asked Judy if she wanted a slice. She did so I dropped two slices down into it. "This is awful. Margo's death has awoken so many emotions. It's really hard sometimes."

Tears flooded my eyes, and I gave into them as they bubbled out and ran down my cheeks.

"Agent Orange consumed his brain that contributed to the mental illness caused from the PTSD. It took control of his mind. Vietnam changed his life and yours too." Judy got up and came over to me and wrapped her arms around me. "Let it all out, sweetie, that's what Margo gave us. A reunion, a new life, free of old hangups and life-long secrets. You've carried your love for Mike for too long, and it got in the way of living. The death of a dear friend gives us freedom to live whatever time we have left of ours. Yes. It's time for you to move on."

I cried for a few more minutes until I pulled away. After blowing my nose and wiping my eyes, I said, "When did you get so smart?"

"About three days ago."

We gave each other another hug, and I buttered our popped-up toast while she refreshed our coffee cups.

"Back to the task at hand," Judy said. "What's in store for today besides a reconfirm of my doctor appointment in the morning."

"What did your attorney say?"

"He said that I'd get my license back sooner if I went for treatment. My department chair said that it's a must or I'll never be able to return. Retirement sounds better and better."

"You need to go to rehab, Judy. Those sessions plant you firmly on the ground and help you to live a normal life again. See how life is through clear eyes."

"I know and will. Carl has mentioned it and says just about the same."

We continued eating as we talked.

"I am tired of working." Judy winked at me. "How do you like retirement?"

"I love it. I come and go. Do what I want. If the weather sucks, I stay indoors. Sometimes, I don't even know what day it is."

"That sounds like a dream." Just at that moment her phone rang. "It's Carl." She answered.

I left the room to give her privacy and turned on my favorite morning news station, *WCCO*. The weather forecast was ending as Judy entered.

"What gives?"

"Carl is taking a few days off. He canceled the flight and is going to drive over here and take me home. He's decided that it's for the best and it'll give us the chance to talk."

"He's so sweet."

"He makes me feel special." Judy smiled.

"You should. He sounds like one-in-a-million." With a twinkle in my eye, I said, "He can stay here."

"Nope. He'll be in a hotel."

"Now for today. It's nine and not too early to call Diane." I looked outside. "Let's give her a call and arrange to go over to talk to her again."

"Go ahead and make the call. I'll get dressed."

"All right. Bring your clothes so we can throw them in the wash."

"I'll get them spinning before we leave. You don't need to do it."

I retrieved my phone, found Diane's number, and called.

"Diane? This is Nancy."

"Oh! How good of you to call. What can I do for you?"

I could almost picture her sinking down on the nearest chair with a puzzled look on her face.

"Are you available in about an hour? Judy and I have a few more questions for you. I assume Will is at work?"

"Yes. He isn't retired. He's alone so I suspect he'll keep working just to have something to do."

"Did he ever marry?"

"Yes. What's this about?"

"We'll tell you when we come. We won't stay long, so don't worry about us, but if you do have some of those lovely, delicious donuts squirreled away in that glass jar and hidden in your kitchen cabinet, we won't turn one down!"

"It's a deal." She chuckled.

"See you soon."

I smiled as I walked down the hallway and stood

outside of the bathroom door and knocked.

"All set," I called through the door.

"Good."

With me wearing a navy-blue sweater set and jeans and Judy in a pair of Sharon's pants and long sleeve turtleneck sweater, we donned our coats and headed out to the garage. Soon we were on the road. I told Judy about the donuts, and she chuckled.

"I remember them. They were yummy."

"My mouth is watering. Do you think she has any?" I asked as I turned onto the main road. "Do you recall for sure if Will was older or younger than Vicky?"

"Oh, is that heart of yours going thumpity-thump?" Judy grinned, wagging a finger at me. "What's on your mind?"

"I'm just curious, that's all. Nothing to it."

"Yeah, well, time will tell."

I kept my thoughts to myself as we traveled to the Storbaekkene house. No, I didn't have romantic thoughts of Will but had found him good-looking. I knew no one could replace Mike, but at least I was beginning to receive confirmation of our mutual love. My heart started to feel open and whole. A release from the past.

The worst part of all this knowledge was that I should've realized it on my own. All these years of wondering and wasting my life. I wondered if it wasn't me? Was I ugly? Was that why he walked away and I didn't get my welcome home kiss? These were questions that still needed answering. Also, why did he have children with someone else when he told me many times he wanted me to be the mother of his children. I was still confused and in the air over these few questions, but at least now the door was open and eventually they'd be answered.

I took a deep breath and shook all thoughts out of my mind. I needed to prepare myself for our meeting with Diane.

"Here we are," I said, parking on the street in front of the house. "It looks the same."

"It does. They say a person can never go back, sometimes I wonder."

"Me too."

We climbed from the car, and I locked it behind me. There were a few steps to climb. Diane opened the door as I went to ring the bell.

When entering the living room, it was as if I was stepping back in time. The furniture was reminiscent of the late sixties, and I was sure the couch was the same as when Vicky was here. The large, comfortable chair would've fit Mr. Storbaekkene. A platform rocker sat in the distant corner with a bag that had knitting needles sticking out from it. Everything appeared as it had so many years ago. The coffee table had a small tray with chocolate and sugar covered donuts upon it.

"You really had donuts," Judy said. "I can't believe it!" She stood leaning over it, ready to take at least one or two.

"Go ahead, you two munchkins. They were in the freezer but should be thawed by now," Diane said.

"Have a seat."

As we each took a donut and bit into it, Diane went after a cup of coffee for each of us.

"They're still to die for," I said.

We each devoured our donut and reached for the second one as she entered with our full coffee cups.

"What's this about, girls?" Diane asked. She reached for a donut and her coffee. "That's Vicky's diary, there on the table. You can take that with the promise of giving it back."

"Of course," Judy said.

"Here's the memory stick with pictures of us as kids. Will can show them to you on his computer," I said.

"You girls are just what I needed. You're always welcome."

"Thanks. We'll always come for donuts," Judy said.

"We were at Minnehaha Falls yesterday and walked around the Home. We did speak with a park ranger about a matter, however, we wondered about Steve Turner. Do you happen to know what his address and phone number are?"

"I'm sure it's in the phone book."

"We're wondering if you think he'll be receptive to talking to us."

"Probably, but dredging up memories is pretty tough," Judy said. "Do you happen to recall the name of the patient who bugged Vicky?"

"There was a man who had mental health problems that liked to follow her around when she looked for her dad."

"That's when I'd be with her. He'd stare at us. What was his name?" I said. "He gave me the creeps."

"Jackson comes to mind."

"At least we have a name," I said. "Can you remember what happened to him? Family?"

"No, not at all."

"Maybe Sharon will find out a few things. She's going through the records today," Judy said. "Tell me, do you recall any missing persons from that time besides Vicky?"

"No. I'm sorry," Diane said, tears filling her eyes.

We finished our donuts, thanked and hugged her before leaving. Judy grabbed the diary.

"Thanks a bunch."

Silently we walked to the car. Once inside, we looked at each other through moist eyes.

"She's alive," Judy said.

"How do you know?"

"My gut tells me so."

Judy
Chapter Thirteen

We headed down the road as I searched for Steve Turner's address. There was something niggling at me, but I wasn't sure what. Then it came to me—

"Did Steve have an older brother?" I looked at Nancy.

"I don't remember much about Steve, but I don't think so. Vicky never mentioned a brother. The diary should give us more clues."

"That's what bugged me. I thought he did have a brother."

I continued searching on my phone for Steve's address and number until I finally discovered it.

"His address is where there used to be cornfields. I'm giving him a call." I pressed the buttons and listened to the ring until at last I left a message and phone number. "We have two phone calls to wait for. Ranger Rick and Steve Turner."

"We're also calling Will again when we have some information to question him about," Nancy said.

She continued our drive toward home.

"Have you heard anything more from Sharon? Is she and her friend coming over tomorrow night?"

"We'll talk with her later," Nancy said.

As we stopped for a light, I answered my ringing

phone. It was the police station.

"This is Detective Johnson from the Minneapolis Police Department."

"Yes, this is Judy Hokstad."

"Is it possible for you and your friend to come by the station within the next hour?"

"We can be there instantly. You just caught us out and about. We'll be right over."

"Good. Stop by the desk and tell the receptionist your name and she'll contact me."

"Okay."

We disconnected.

"Head to the police station and we're to see Detective Johnson. That's the orders," I said. "He sounds like a nice guy. Now we can compare your diary and Vicky's once we're home."

"So far, we haven't really come across much," Nancy said. She went around the block and started driving toward the Lake Street station. "We should have my diary along for him to peruse."

"We'll tell him about it. I'm sure Vicky's has been read and reread a dozen times. Memorized."

As Nancy drove toward the station, I watched the houses go by and thought of my years growing up in this metropolis. In the day, it wasn't nearly as large or populated as it was now. Families only had one car but now there were generally two or more that made parking tough. It was that way all over the country, I presumed.

I thought about our times as kids, taking the city bus to downtown and going shopping. Our shopping was more like, "look and see." We couldn't afford anything. Nancy, maybe once in a while, but she sewed most of her attire. I wasn't that talented. Mine, Margo's, and Sharon's clothes were hand-me-downs. I was lucky in that I had girl cousins who wore cool clothes they gave me once they tired of the article. We wore the same thing to school for a couple days in a row and then wore the next outfit for the same length of time. We wore our Sunday best dresses to church. While in grade school, I wore little white gloves on Sunday. Once I started in junior high school, gloves were out of fashion. However, we wore dresses in school. The code didn't allow for girls to wear pants. We'd walk to school and change our clothes if that was in order. No pants in school. Period. I was thinking about our physical education classes and the uniforms we had to wear and picturing my mom ironing the blue shorts and my white blouse as Nancy parked.

"You've been quiet, what's on your mind?" she said, shutting off the car.

"Honey, you don't want to know. It'll only add years on you." I sighed and opened the car door to get out. "I'm glad we're working on this puzzle."

"I am too."

Once we entered the police station, I gave the woman behind the bars my name and filled out a short form requesting personal information and the reason for being there. When I'd completed the form and turned it in, I sat beside Nancy to wait.

"I feel like we're in jail," Nancy whispered.

"We are."

Within a few minutes, Johnson stood in the open doorway and requested us to follow him to his office.

"Here's my home away from home. Have a seat, ladies," he said. He motioned to the two empty chairs before sitting in his behind the desk. "I would like for both of you to introduce yourself and then give me a brief rundown of your relationship with Vicky Storbaekkene."

"Judy Hokstad. Doctor Judy Hokstad. I teach German studies in Madison at the university. However, yes, it was I who rolled the car on Friday night, and that's why I might still have the raccoon look. I've known Vicky for the same length of time as my friend, Nancy." I took a breath before continuing with my saga of childhood and playtime, dates and movies.

"Sounds good," Johnson said. He dotted his i's and crossed his t's on his notepad, then said, "Next."

"Nancy Bjork. My story is almost identical to Judy's except that I taught school for a number of years and am now retired. I went with Vicky a few times to visit her dad at the Soldiers' Home and there was always this one patient that gave me the creeps. That's why we decided to walk around earlier yesterday, just to get a feel of the park. Neither of us had been there for quite some time."

"You both found a rock similar to a cemetery stone? Or a depression in front of one?"

"Yes. Ranger Rick must've pointed them out to you?" Cocking my head, I said, "Did you go and look?"

"As a matter of fact, I have. Another officer and myself walked the area. We're going back through old records." He leaned back in his chair and glanced from Nancy to myself and back to Nancy. "Who found the first one?"

"Me."

"What caught your eye?"

"I don't like admitting this, but I fell down and couldn't get up. I ended up on all fours and pulling myself up on a tree to standing. That gave me a different perspective of the land." I grinned. "If something stupid is going to happen, leave it to me."

"That would make you notice," Johnson said, taking notes.

"Honestly, Judy. Admitting it to a detective? I would've kept it secret from sheer embarrassment." Nancy giggled.

"What about you?" Johnson looked at Nancy with his pen in hand.

"Nothing that notable. The stone looked odd compared to the other surrounding rocks. That's all."

"Thank you ladies. Before we pursue any of these leads, I have to ask if you have anything else to add?"

"Our mutual friend passed away. Another friend was the minister. Saturday was the funeral. Sharon is going to look into the Soldiers' Home records. She didn't know Vicky as a kid, just us two. Mrs. Storbaekkene attended our friend's funeral then later came to Sharon's with Will, Vicky's brother."

"I had thought of putting together a memory stick of photos for our deceased friend's daughter and since have found a number of photos with Vicky in them. We gave Diane a copy today and a few other miscellaneous pictures," Nancy said. "Did you know that there was a patient at the Soldiers' Home that used to bug Vicky? I'm not sure of his name, I think it was Jackson, but he followed her around a lot when she'd go to see her dad."

"Another thing we didn't know about. I never knew about this patient, it's not anywhere," Detective Johnson said, scratching his hair. "Why didn't you two come forward before? I didn't read your names as witnesses."

"Too young to know what anything is about," I said. "Too busy going to parties. I suppose I thought that she'd appear."

"I would guess that I thought the same thing."

"You don't have your diary with you, do you?" Johnson said.

"No," Nancy said, shaking her head. "I can go and get it and bring it to you?"

"Diane, Mrs. Storbaekkene, gave us Vicky's diary right before we came here." I waited a moment. "I thought we could go through it and compare it with Nancy's. You know? Inconsistencies type of thing."

"Well, ladies, I'd like for you to leave both with me, if you will."

"I'll go and fetch Vicky's," Nancy said. She got up and looked out into the hallway and said, "Oh dear."

"Hold on. It's a maze to try and figure out because of all the partitions." Johnson snagged a uniformed officer in the hallway to escort her to the main entrance with orders to wait for her return and bring her back to his office.

"I think she's alive." I had waited for him to return to his chair. "It's my gut instinct. What leads do you have? Any?"

"What we have has led us nowhere. You two have caused us to consider reopening the case and take a closer look."

"She was a good person. Her family deserves closure."

"They all do."

"Someone should've coughed up useful information by now."

We heard approaching footsteps.

"Here," Nancy said, handing the diary to him. "I'll either be by later today or tomorrow will drop mine off."

"Give me your address and I'll have someone stop by to pick it up."

Nancy gave him the needed information.

Shortly afterward, we were in the car and heading for home.

"What did you two talk about when I went for Vicky's diary?"

"I asked about leads and he sounded like there weren't any new ones. Then I said that I think she's alive and also that the family should have closure."

"What did he say about you thinking Vicky is alive?" Nancy said.

"Nothing."

"Nothing? What does that mean? Does he agree

with you or not?"

"I wish I knew."

Nancy
Chapter Fourteen

As I drove home, I glanced over at Judy and realized her eyes were shut and her head was leaning backward. She was taking a snooze. I hoped it would work out for her once she returned home—that her department chair would be sympathetic but most of all Carl would be. I prayed he'd take good care of her. It sounded as if he would, I told myself, but looks were deceiving. The lawyers and the driving laws wouldn't be easy on her either, I suspected. *It's too bad the accident happened or was it? Now she'll be forced into treatment.* As I turned into my driveway and opened the garage door with a magic push of the button, Judy whispered something.

"What?"

"Huh? Oh nothing. I must've still been dreaming," Judy said. "Let's get inside before the police get here."

"Yeah. I've never had a police car parked in front of my house. The neighbors might talk," I said. I grabbed my purse and climbed from the car. Judy followed.

"I've got a bad headache all of a sudden," Judy said. She massaged her temples. "I'd like to curl up for a little while."

"Go ahead. I'm taking my diary and making copies

of the last two weeks before Vicky disappeared." I started for the bedroom. "You can use whatever is on the couch. I'm afraid of not having this done before the policeman arrives."

"It's a great idea. Don't worry about me."

As Judy made herself comfy and cozy on the couch, I took the diary and went upstairs to my office where the copier/printer was located and my computer. Fortunately, I'd purchased a new ink cartridge because now I might need it.

It took close to fifteen minutes before I'd finished with the project. I went ahead and made copies of the few days directly after the disappearance, hoping it would give me a feel of the climate and my feelings about the aftermath. My parents were always afraid and Mom, especially, had a terrible time letting me out of her sight. Dad drove me to work and picked me up more often than ever before this abduction happened. However, after a few months when the news reports had shifted to other stories and Vicky's abduction was rarely spoken of or reported, they began to relinquish their control and rules over me.

I'd hoped for a relationship from my soldier boy, but Mike had other ideas and after a year or two, I became engaged. No longer did I think about Vicky, it's sad to say. Judy, Margo, Sharon, and I should've started a search party over the years or done what we could to keep her memory alive. Prayer vigils and gathering classmates would've helped with the investigation. I wished I could go back in time and make all this right for her memory and for the family.

I'd made the copies and set them aside and took the diary back to the coffee table before throwing Sharon and Judy's clothes into the washing machine. Judy needed covering, so I took care of it and brushed the hair from her forehead. When the washing machine was going, I gave Sharon a call.

"Hey, Sharon. Are you busy?"

"I've got about a minute and a half," she said. "I have only a few minutes left of my allotted time at the Soldier's Home."

"Oh! Well, can you come out after you're finished?"

"Yes. I have your address. I'll be there in 30-40 minutes."

"It's a deal."

We disconnected and I made myself a cup of hot chocolate. I wondered what to make for supper? Myself, I was satisfied with a poached egg, but what would Judy like? Sharon may also be here. It was time to be creative. I let the chocolate finish melting in the cup and went downstairs to the freezer to retrieve a frozen dish of lasagna. I also took a large roast upstairs with me. Roasts were easy, thaw and pop in the oven with carrots, potatoes, and onions. It would suffice for the remaining time with Judy.

Upstairs, I slipped the aluminum lasagna pan into the oven and placed the roast on a plate and inside of the refrigerator. With the mug of hot chocolate in hand, I went out to the living room to sit and relax. My relax time didn't last long before I noticed a black car park in my driveway and a man climbing out who looked suspiciously like an undercover policeman. I took the diary and went to the front door before he could ring the bell and wake Judy.

"Hello," I said, opening it as he reached for the doorbell. "Are you from the police department?"

"Yes. Officer Quist." He showed his badge. "I'm here for a diary."

"Here." He held out a bag and I dropped the diary inside. "You're checking it for prints."

"Following orders. You never know what may be revealed."

"True."

"Thanks. Detective Johnson will be in touch."

He turned to walk away, and I went back inside to resume drinking my hot chocolate. I drank it down and scraped the bottom for chocolate remnants before leaning back in my recliner chair. Fortunately, I was able to get in a brief snooze before Sharon arrived. Judy woke at the same time.

"Two sleeping beauties, I see?" Sharon winked, holding her briefcase. "I think I'll join you."

"Hi, come on in. We're just making hot chocolate," I said. "Sharon, show me what's in your briefcase before I make you a cup."

"You made fresh hot chocolate? I haven't had that since I was a kid," Judy said.

"I used a piece of *Ghirardelli* caramel/chocolate in a cup filled with milk and microwaved for 85 seconds. It's heavenly," I said.

"You two look about dead to the world. I'll fix it," Sharon said. "Judy, do you want a cup and do you want another, Nancy?"

"I'd love one." Judy yawned. "It might put me back to sleep."

"I could go for another." I handed Sharon my mug and sat up. She removed the relevant papers and handed them over. "Thanks."

"Did you find the name Jackson anywhere?" Judy called.

"Wait! I can't hear over the microwave," Sharon said.

I perused the papers Sharon had given me. Jackson's name was listed as deceased, but that wasn't a surprise. Jackson Gunderson. Birth date: 6/1/ 1935. Death date: 12/24/2005. Jackson came from a small town in central Minnesota near Fergus Falls and was buried in the cemetery in the Lutheran cemetery. His discharge date wasn't listed but it said he'd left without returning one day. The final day of his documented whereabouts was 5/15/1970.

"That's prom night!" Judy said. "He had to have abducted her."

Sharon carried in two hot mugs and went back for hers before sitting near Judy on the couch, both covered with the same blanket.

"I just read on here that Jackson was never discharged. He was never found."

"The date is the same as the prom," Judy said. "It's also as if he disappeared."

"Exactly," Sharon said. "What are you two thinking?"

"Where was he from?" Judy asked.

"Fergus Falls. Sort of near Glenwood," Sharon said. "There's several small towns in that area."

"The information fits," I said. "I think it's worth looking into."

"I wonder if the police haven't already?" Sharon said. She blew on her hot chocolate. "What am I saying? They already have. Why wouldn't they have?"

"What if they didn't know about him?" Judy said. "What if the information wasn't forthcoming? What if the hospital thought he'd just wandered off and that he fell into the creek? It's entirely possible."

"You think she's alive, don't you?" Sharon said. She sipped from her cup. "This is really good."

"I do," Judy said. She stirred her drink and took a swallow. "This is yummy."

"It might not even be the same Jackson, you know?" I said.

"It is. I can feel it," Judy said.

"Right. In your gut," I said.

"Judy? If you're right, we'll celebrate," Sharon said.

"I'll pay for it, too," Judy said.

"How long can you stay?" I asked Sharon. "I have a pan of lasagna in the oven."

"That sounds good. Peggy will be able to make it tomorrow night, if the invitation is still on the table."

"Sounds good and Carl might be here, also," I said.

"Now it sounds like old times," Sharon said. "Together and having fun."

"Yes. No more drinking and chasing around."

"Good for you!" Sharon said. "Will you make things right with Carl?"

"In my heart, I pray for it."

"Then it will happen."

I moved to sit beside them and we each read the copied diary entrants.

"I'm so sorry Mike couldn't escort you," Sharon said. "Your heart sure longed for him."

"Look what you have written here," Judy said. She read: *Mom made me go with Vicky to see her dad at work. I didn't want to because of that man. Mom said to go and be with Vicky.*

"Why did she have to go on that particular time? Any idea?" Judy asked.

"I've wondered that myself." I took a deep breath. "Her dad would forget his lunch and Vicky would bring it to him on Saturdays, if he was working."

"Let's search what day this was," Sharon said. She finished her hot chocolate. "That hit the spot."

"Yeah, it did," Judy said. She had her phone in hand and was searching for the relevant date and day. "It was a Friday."

"Shoot. That knocks that theory out," I said. "Maybe it was school conferences and there wasn't any school?"

"I honestly don't remember," Sharon said. "It could have been."

"Well, we're stuck," Judy said. "If I didn't have to go back home, I'd say we should take a short trip to Fergus Falls."

"Let's search the web," I said. "We should be able

to find an address and possibly a phone number."

Judy placed her palms on either side of her temples. "I still have a headache."

"I'll get the aspirin," I said. "What time do we see the doctor?"

"Nine-thirty."

"What did the doctor say about headaches or how much rest you should be getting?" Sharon asked.

"I'm just tired and want my own pillow," Judy said and took the offered aspirin. "Thanks." After swallowing the pills, she said, "He told me to take it easy and we have been. I wasn't prescribed any meds for anything. I get tired really easily."

"Searching for Vicky has been tough and that falling down was hard on you. I suspect you're still achy and sore from the accident," I said. "And, I've expected too much from you, not giving you time to relax."

"Listen you two, I'm doing fine." Judy's phone dinged. "A message from Carl. He's half-way here and will be by in the morning to take me to the doctor."

"Nope. That ain't gonna happen without me," I said.

"Oh yeah?"

"Yeah, and me too," Sharon said.

"Honestly, you two are hopeless," Judy said, chuckling.

"You're not getting rid of us that easily," I said. "We've been without each other for too long." I grinned and gave Judy a hug.

Sharon joined in on the hug. When we broke apart, we wiped our eyes dry.

"I've never admitted my sexual orientation to anyone from the congregation. No one. It's been terribly hard to live a lie," Sharon said. "I need to come forward but am afraid."

"Honey, people will always love you for who you are," Judy said.

"You two have given me strength," Sharon said. "I've needed that for many years."

"Me, too," Judy said. "I didn't know how much I needed my old friends until now. I do hope Carl still loves me in spite of all that's happened between us."

"He sees your inner soul and accepts you for who you are," I said.

"Yes, but he can't live with me."

"Times are changing, Judy. There have been many prayers sent and you've been working your way to this moment. Today isn't tomorrow and in twenty-four hours, your thoughts will be different. Time changes all."

"Yes and I know you're right."

"Tell us about Carl," Sharon said.

"He says he'll be here straight away in the morning, and I should have my suitcase packed. He'll take me to the doctor and he wants to be able to speak with him about my injuries. After, he'll drive me home. He wants to spend time alone with me and apologizes for being so possessive, but there are matters that need my attention."

"That's good, though," Sharon said. "He's looking

out for you. I'm happy about that."

"Sharon's right. He has your best interests at heart."

"You're probably both right. So, you'll have to wait to see him again. Sharon, tell us what you plan to do about your situation? Anything? Nothing?"

Sharon got up and walked to the front window and stood facing the outside. She took a few long breaths before turning and looking at us.

"I'll probably have to resign."

"What will you do?" I asked.

"I've given it an awful lot of thought and plan to set up an appointment with the bishop next month. You two have given me the courage to continue with my journey." Sharon nodded to us. "You see? How beautiful is life? It's time to live the life we were born to live, that God has given us." She moved toward us. "Let's eat. I'm starved!"

"I'll check on the food."

"Let's put some music on and relax."

"I'm setting the table," Sharon said, "but not before I contact Peggy."

"What about the bishop?"

"You're right. He's first."

I busied myself by getting a small salad put together while Judy helped after finding the music stations on the TV, one that played soft jazz.

When the food was ready to place on the table, Sharon joined us.

"The appointment is made."

"That's good news, isn't it?" I said.

"I'm scared. Really, really scared." Sharon sunk into the nearest chair, crying. "What have I done?"

"You've started a new phase in your life," I said.

"And it's scary. Scary as hell," Judy said.

Judy
Chapter Fifteen

"Let's eat," Nancy said. "Come on, Sharon. The food will take your mind from your troubles."

"I doubt that, but it may help," I said. Sharon looked a bit dazed. In my olden days, four days ago, I would've offered her a bump. A good strong jolt of whiskey would've knocked all of her fears away, and she'd feel refreshed and would have the nerve to tell the bishop and her congregation to go and screw themselves. Those days were gone. "A new phase. New life. New everything, Sharon. We need to go shopping. That's what's in order!"

"Leave it to Judy to come up with a solution," Nancy said. "I wish I had thought of it myself, instead of you." She smiled at me. "You always know what will tickle us and relieve any pressure we've put upon ourselves."

"I think Judy knows because she's been hurting inside for so many years," Sharon said. She took a bite and waited to finish, "Just like me."

"I am right here, you know. You two don't need to talk around me."

"We know, we're just letting you know how much we appreciate you," Nancy said.

"I wish Margo could've joined us. Wouldn't that

have been a trip!"

"Have you spoken to your attorney?" Nancy asked. She snagged a slice of garlic bread and began eating it.

"As a matter of fact, I have, but he's not the kind of attorney who would be good for this type of situation."

"Oh dear," Sharon said, setting her fork down on the plate. "Now what?"

"Carl should have names and numbers when he arrives," I said. "Let's talk about other matters such as shopping. Sharon, I love you and your clothes, but really? They're frumpy."

"Really? You don't say?"

"Yes, I say. Furthermore, so are mine. It's now or never with my credit card. We haven't been to the Mall of America."

"It's expensive there," Nancy said.

"You can buy books, we'll hunt for clothes." To Sharon, I said, "Well? What do you think?"

"Sure, but only one item. My card is almost maxed out."

"So's mine."

"Me too, but so what? It's our new life phase. Let's go for it full-blast."

We finished our meal and soon had the dishwasher loaded. Sharon and I held each other close before putting on our jackets to go and Nancy soon joined us.

"Should we drive together? Let me drive," Sharon said. "It's my pleasure after this lovely meal and then we'll be here tomorrow night. Nancy, you've done an awful lot."

"If you don't mind?"

"Nope."

We climbed into Sharon's SUV, with me sitting in the back. For some reason, I kept getting more tired, like I hadn't slept. Seated in the backseat gave me an opportunity to shut my eyes for a few minutes. Nancy lived approximately a half-hour from the shopping mall. Sharon was lucky. When she'd parked, I opened my eyes to us parked right outside of Macy's. It was great and I felt good too, the short nap gave me the extra energy to pursue shopping.

"I want shoes." We entered the door located right near the shoe department, and my eyes opened wide with wonder. "It's like it's a Divine Order to have these beautiful shoes right in front of my nose."

"Honestly Judy, you and shoes have always teamed up. Remember those red shoes with the big ribbon on top when we were in junior high? We all swooned over them," Nancy said. She shook her head.

"I couldn't believe you, dancing at school dances wearing spikes. How could you stand up? I would've tipped over, fallen into a lump or else into the punch bowl," Sharon said.

"Never mind, you two curmudgeons, I'm getting another pair. It'll give me the strength and courage to face the judge and judgement day."

"We're right with you."

After trying on five different shapes, sizes and styles, I thought of purchasing the first pair. Six-inch heels, half navy blue, the other, white."

"It's not snazzy enough," Sharon said, looking down at my feet. "You need more zip."

"We don't want to give the judge a bad impression or make him too dizzy from too much zip from my shoe design." I sighed and picked up the second pair that had purple and pink zig-zag lines running through them with a scarlet red coloring. I went to purchase them.

"Now for Sharon," Nancy said.

"Let's walk out into the mall," Sharon said.

"Hold on and let me run these out to the car," I said. "Keys?"

I hurried out to the car, and when I went back inside, they were over by women's clothing.

"We should go to Victoria's Secret. If you bought a bra from there and wore it when you spoke to the bishop and the congregation, you'd feel like a different person. One of those sexy things. Your friend would like it, too."

"You're a bit crazy, sometimes, Judy. Has anyone ever told you that?" Sharon said, chuckling. "You're silly."

"She does have a point, though. It's either underwear or she'll have you purchasing a sexy dress. I think you'd prefer the bra and panties." Nancy grinned. "I agree, though, our Judy does have crazy ideas."

"There's nothing crazy about it. We need love and laughter in our lives more now than ever before. When we were youngsters or young adults, we thought we knew everything and thought everyone would love us. What's not to love, you know? And now here we are, searching for love, searching for laughter. We can depend on each other for many reasons but the basic reason that we are able to depend upon each other, is that we loved each other so many years ago. Because of the intimate knowledge, we can express ourselves clearly and honestly." I paused for a moment. "Don't you get it? We need to uplift each other as we enter our new life phase."

"Yes, teacher," Sharon said. "I know. And we will. You might be right about the underwear."

"I'm the teacher, remember?" Nancy said. "I could use one of those bras and panties."

"What about you and Carl? Bet your undies are natty," Sharon said. She cocked her head and raised a brow in a question mark. "Right? You must be prepared for all things."

"You're right. I need undies. Let's go!"

We had to walk down a few lanes and study the map until we actually found the store. The store clerks headed us in the right direction.

"I can't believe I'm doing this," Nancy whispered. "I don't even have a boyfriend."

"It's for, 'just in case,'" I said. "You'll be ready. I might not be around to lead you here."

"I love this one. It has lace in all the right places," Sharon said.

"This one here, shows less than that one does," I said. "You should try it on."

"I can help myself," Sharon said. She took the bra

in her size and panties. "No way are you two co
in with me. I don't want anyone to faint when they see my weight gain."

"Don't worry, hon, no one's going to see all my lumps," Nancy said. She held two scant bras and panties.

"No one is going to laugh at my bat-winged arms," I said.

With our underwear in hand, we entered three separate stalls to try them on. There were plenty of moans and groans until we carried our finds to the front desk to pay for them.

"Now what?" Nancy said.

We stepped out into the walkway.

"Yes, Judy, lead us onward."

"You mean, astray."

"That's already happened," Nancy said.

"Coffee and then home."

The nearest coffee house wasn't far, so we each had a cup and enjoyed the passersby.

"It's been a good evening," Sharon said. "I never would've bought these for myself. You're right Judy. I'm going to wear these and they'll give me pleasure."

"I'm not sure when I'll wear mine," Nancy said, "but who knows? My time might be right around the corner and look at the fun I'll have with them. How about you?"

"I'm hoping that someday soon, Carl and I will be back together. I'm finally thinking with a straight head. This trip here for Margo, the accident, all of it has really shook me up. I never realized what kind of drunk and pot smoker I was. I wonder how I could've kept my job all these years?"

"Honey, you're facing it and Carl will always stand by you," Nancy said.

"Call me if you need anything at all, Judy. I'll come running," Sharon said. "You've helped me to see where I need to go on my life's journey. You're my guardian angel."

"Oh no! Don't put all that on my shoulders. I have enough of my own to care for."

When finished with our coffee, we went to the car. Sharon drove us to Nancy's and she left for home right away.

"I'm pooped," Nancy said.

"Me, too."

We both went our separate ways and it wasn't long before I'd fallen asleep. I woke with the shakes again and went to the bathroom. I wanted a drink so bad I could almost taste it. I tiptoed down the hallway and thought I was quiet as I opened and closed cabinets in search of a bottle of whiskey. I found one! The stash was above the refrigerator. Climbing down, I tripped and landed on the floor with a broken bottle beside me and whiskey running across the floor.

I looked up to a bright light and a scream.

"What were you doing? Shame on you!"

"Will you help me up, at least?"

"No. Get up yourself. Now I have to clean this mess up."

"No, you don't. I have to clean this mess up, not you. Go back to bed and pretend you didn't see any of it." I managed to pull myself up to standing. I noticed a steady stream of blood coming from a few scratches. "Go and I'm fine." I took a tissue to wipe the blood and prevent any more bleeding. It worked. I knew the doctor tomorrow would have to take a closer look to make sure there wasn't an infection or imbedded glass shards.

"Positive?"

"Yes. I don't want you to see me anymore like this."

She did an about face, which I was grateful for. I was mad at myself. *I thought I had it under control but my body needs cleansing. Mom? Where are you? I need help. Why am I thinking of her? She was a drunk and so was Dad, my genetic makeup was filled with alcoholism. I wanted my mother's arms around me. I'm a big girl, why am I sobbing? I only want to be loved and be lovable.*

I found the mop and broom and began the cleanup. I hoped for several more hours of sleep. Humming softly to myself, I sang an old hymn from childhood, "Jesus Loves Me," as I worked. Peace began to flow through me. After the cleanup, I went upstairs and took a shower before going back to bed.

Consequences for my actions from many years of drinking. The Piper was being paid.

The next morning neither of us spoke much, and I was very happy when the front door bell rang, knowing Carl was on the other side of the door.

"I'm going but don't worry about me, Carl's here."

"I hate to see you go," Nancy said. She wiped her eyes.

"Thank you Nancy for everything." I set my suitcase down and gave her a big hug. "I'll let you know how it goes."

"I apologize for being mad last night," Nancy said. She smiled. "Please forgive me. You're going through an awful lot and I should've known better."

"It's forgiven. I'll text you with updates." I blew her a kiss.

Carl met me right as I stepped outside the door.

"Hi," I said, tears filling my eyes.

"Nancy, it's nice seeing you again," Carl said.

"Yes, and you too," Nancy said. "Have a safe trip."

"Judy, you're no worse for wear," Carl said. He placed his arm behind my back. "You look sad?" When I nodded, he said, "Tell me."

I followed along to the car.

Once inside of it and buckled up, Carl said, "What happened?"

Should I expose myself again as a drunk? How will that effect our relationship?

"I don't care for your silence and the way in which you stare out of the side window. What happened between you and Nancy?"

"I'm afraid to tell you."

"You need to spit it out, Judy, or you'll never get anywhere."

"I know."

"Have you spoken to your department chair?"

"Yes, and she isn't very happy."

"I don't suppose so." Carl clutched the steering wheel as if it would steer itself. "Where to? What exit?"

"The next one. Right down to 38th St. That's where his office is located. The building used to be a *Jolly's* toy store and is now a clinic."

"I want to know now, Judy, no surprises in the doctor's office. Not like before when you were found with a bottle in your side pocket. Tell me."

"Well, okay." I breathed deeply and let it out before beginning my story about the event during the night. "That's all."

"What else are you not telling me? I feel as if there is something you're hiding."

"I dumped out my flask immediately once able to but before bed, I tried to suck out a drop and was bummed because of it being emptied."

"There. That's good. You're finally being honest with me." Carl glanced over at me. "Finally. I've waited years for this to happen. Let's see if it'll continue and how far we can go."

"Do you mean with our relationship?"

"Of course. What else would it be?"

"I need help, Carl."

"That's the first step."

Carl parked while I gathered my thoughts. I hoped the doctor would deem me fit to go home. He should allow it since I wasn't the driver.

"Thanks." I smiled at Carl.

"Promise honesty from here on out?"

"It's a deal. You're too good to me."

"All right." Carl gave me a quick kiss before he opened the door.

As we walked inside of the building, I thought of what had just passed between us. It warmed my heart. I checked in at the main desk and we found a seat to wait. My thoughts drifted to Carl. He was so sweet and kind. Why hadn't I straightened up before it was too late? Sighing, I looked around me and thought about how nice it had been married to Carl. He was still good to me. He'd been a good husband. I never took away his keys after the divorce and I got the house. Why would I when he still treated me like a queen.

My name was called and Carl followed me into the doctor's office.

Dr. Berg gave me a general look over and asked a multitude of questions. He didn't like the few headaches I'd had and said I should see my own physician if they persisted. I knew why they happened, it was withdrawal symptoms and they probably would worsen. I was in a hurry to get home. We thanked him and went to the car.

"I need to get home right away and see my doctor." I frowned. "The headaches and I've had the shakes. It'll only worsen."

"Let's go and get a bite," Carl said. He started the car.

"There's a diner not far from here, near the Riverview Theater."

"Show me the way."

I told him where to turn, and soon were parked outside of the diner.

We climbed from the car and went across the street

to the coffee house. The smell of fresh brewed coffee made my toes tingle and nose twitch. We each ordered a bowl of Scandinavian creamy vegetable soup.

"I know I'm home in Minne-so-ta—when the menus state Scandinavian soup."

"You betcha!" Carl said. "I think we need to check you into a hospital immediately, Judy, to get this taken care of. You need treatment. You're starting down a spiral staircase, and it's only going to get worse. You need nursing care and also a mental health professional to see you through all the trauma you've experienced and never dealt with."

"I'm afraid."

"As well you should be." Carl ate some of his soup as did I.

"I'd thought about going for treatment again. The last time didn't work. I must not have been ready."

"You are now. I can tell. We're finally on the same page."

While we ate, I texted Nancy and Sharon to tell them the doctor visit went quite well and that the doctor said for me to go home right away. "I should retire. My retirement is good. I can live on it."

"We'll retire together once this is cleared up. I got the name of a good attorney for you." Carl reached for his phone. "I'm calling someone who can represent you. She also took care of a friend's kid who was stuck in a similar situation."

"Okay." I felt comforted from all of Carl's help. He knew an awful lot of people and was very well liked. I sipped the remnants of my coffee and listened as he spoke to the receptionist. "Done. You can call her tomorrow or when we get home. It'll be a different person than I'd hoped for, but she'll be just as good."

My phone dinged a message and it was from Nancy. As I began to read it, Sharon answered. Nancy's read: *I'm glad all is well with you and the doctor said you're free to go home. I'll take care of Sharon's clothes. Love you Nancy.* Sharon's message read much the same: *You know what's best for you. Take care of yourself. Call me if it gets to be too hard and painful. Love you. Sharon.*

My reply: *You two are heaven sent. Thank you. Love and kisses. Judy.*

I looked over at Carl and gave him a huge smile. "I'm visiting the ladies room, I'll be right back."

As soon as I returned, Carl said, "Ready for the drive home?"

"You betcha."

We walked arm in arm out to the car.

"I don't want to screw it up," I said. "I need you in my next stage to direct me."

"Don't worry. I know what entrance and exit you need. Right now, you're heading for the best part of your life, the third act."

Nancy
Chapter Sixteen

Shame on me for feeling relieved when Judy left earlier than expected. Another night with her in the house would've kept me up with worry about her well-being. What was she thinking? Did she really need the liquor that desperately? Apparently, she did. How awful for her. My heart went to her with prayers that she'd make it through the treatment. Withdrawals, I'd heard, could be pretty awful and downright deadly if not for proper care. Carl seemed to care deeply for her otherwise he wouldn't have driven here for the sole purpose of taking her to the doctor's appointment and back home to Madison. He'd taken a few days off from work for this road trip, and I hoped Judy didn't screw it up. You never knew with her. I'd like to see those two back together again. He had to have been deeply in love with her when they split, why else would he have never remarried? Judy was lucky to have someone who loved her so desperately.

I wished I did. I wished someone loved me with all his heart and soul. Had Mike loved me that deeply? I thought he had. I could see breaking an engagement because of an illness but what else did he suffer from besides PTSD? Wouldn't my love for him have pulled him through and kept our marriage together? I wished the answers would be forthcoming because I felt lost and lonesome without anyone to cling to on dark nights or hold me when I needed loving.

My thoughts switched to the matter at hand. I sent a text to Sharon: *Dinner served at 7. Is Peggy still coming?*

I went about my business and put the roast in the oven with a few onions, salt and pepper. While it baked, I set aside the needed potatoes and carrots to have ready. About the time I received a response from Sharon, I was ready to mix up a fresh broccoli salad with celery, raisins, and sunflower seeds.

Sharon responded: *Peg's fixed up a nice desert. We'll be there about 6:30. Don't do anything special, friendship is the main ingredient.*

I couldn't push Mike from my mind. I'd never been able to. Now his beloved sister and her guest were coming for dinner. Why couldn't he be by my side? It would've been so much fun.

I wish she was my sister-in-law.

I had a marriage and threw it away because of not shaking Mike from my mind. Being able to talk about him helped. It helped to clarify my thoughts and feelings. Why has it taken so long for Sharon to accept Mike's death?

Sharon must love deeply. Did Mike love like that also? Is that how he loved me? Then why split?

I had to discover the answer so I could ease my mind and find peace from the love I felt.

Since the table was set, and I'd taken care of setting out the needed bowls and everything else was lined up, I took a break. The albums still sat on the coffee table and I opened them up. There we all were again. My eyes moistened, but it was comforting to look at the pictures and think about our lives, how we'd changed but still were the same inside. The city had changed. Minnehaha Falls sure didn't look the same because of the new parking lot and walking restrictions. The falls themselves held wonder and majesty. In an odd way, time stood still at the falls. Families still arrived there with picnic baskets, young couples still strolled hand-in-hand. I wondered how I fit into the scheme of things? Where was my life heading? Alone? Crotchety and lonesome. That was how the last stage of my life would be if I didn't change.

Why hadn't I given this a thought a long time ago?

I got up to add the vegetables to the roaster and went back to sit, carrying a hot cup of tea. It tasted good, and I sat so I could stare out of the window and watch the cars go by. I turned the news on, picked up the albums again and began riffling through the pages. My cell phone rang, and I answered it.

"Hello? Will, is this you?"

"Yes." Will cleared his throat. "I, um, are you busy tonight? I have something to show you."

"Sharon and her friend are coming for dinner. How about later?"

"That would work. What time?"

"Eight or eight-thirty." I didn't think he had my address so I gave it to him.

"Thanks. I'll see you later."

"Sounds good."

After disconnecting, I wondered why I hadn't invited him to dinner. Will wasn't married, I was pretty sure of that. I sent Sharon a message since I wanted her opinion. It read: *What's your thoughts of inviting Will for supper? He has something to show us and I'd said later to show up. Should I ring him back with a dinner invite?*

Almost immediately, she responded: *Yes, of course!*

Before I lost my nerve, I rang him up.

"Will? It's Nancy again." I felt my cheeks turning red from nervousness.

"Yes? You're not canceling out on me, are you?"

"Nope. I'm inviting you for dinner. I should've to begin with. Dinner's at seven, come earlier if you choose."

"Thanks and I will be there. Shall I bring a bottle of wine?"

"That would be lovely. We're having a beef roast."

"Sounds good."

We disconnected with me smiling. It'd been so many years since I'd sat and had dinner with a man, I couldn't remember the last time. I wondered what to do next then decided it was time to add another serving to the table.

After, it occurred to me that a little makeup might be in order. Down the hall, I walked to the bedroom. I couldn't wear these old jeans. I didn't have any earrings on. I changed into a new pair of jeans and a pale blue sweater set. I added a colorful scarf around my neck and pinned it with a broach depicting the season—a cornucopia filled with pumpkins and gourds. With matching earrings, I was satisfied. Next, I took care of makeup, adding a berry shade of lipstick. I was ready.

I felt a little twinge as I walked to the kitchen. Was I ready to impress another man? Was that what I was doing? Flirting? Honestly, I didn't know after all this time.

Car doors slammed at the right time, taking my mind from the situation. "Here goes," I said to myself and took a deep breath.

At the door stood Sharon and Peggy. Introductions were made, and I was happy to see a sparkle in Sharon's eye and could understand why. Peggy's warm smile made me think of a warm, cozy cup of tea or coffee with a plate of chocolate chip cookies. Peggy handed me a spray of fall flowers.

"Thanks! How nice! Come on in," I said. "Make yourself at home."

"Nancy, you look great. New look?" Sharon grinned. "Anything new and exciting beneath the top layer?"

"Sharon! My word. I'd expect that from Judy but not you." I smiled. "Nope. Saving it for the right time."

"I was curious." Sharon began removing her coat.

"What's that about?" Peggy glanced from Sharon to me.

"I'm sure Sharon will tell you all about it sooner or later."

Sharon hung both coats while I filled a vase full of water for the flowers. They were purple asters, yellow chrysanthemum's, and yellow pansies and were absolutely beautiful.

"All that's left for me to do is make the gravy."

"I'll cut the meat and dish up the vegetables," Sharon said.

"I'll help wherever it's needed," Peggy added.

"You're a guest so relax, but you can answer the door when Will arrives."

Sharon and I took care of the food while Peggy found four wine glasses and rinsed them out to have ready for use. Will arrived at the right moment.

"Come in," I called. "Make yourself at home."

Will entered the kitchen and looked around.

Sharon and I finished setting the food on the table while Peggy made sure the water glasses were filled. Prayers were said before we began.

"I have a box with some of my boyhood treasures inside." Will took a bite. "I wanted to go through them with you and Sharon or Judy. I'm hoping it'll evoke unexplored memories."

"Good. When we're finished eating, we'll do that."

"I don't want to disrupt any of your plans," Will said. He set his fork down and held out the wine bottle. "My! I'm at the head of the table. Should I pour?"

"By all means."

"We have many things to discuss tonight, least of all, getting to know each other," Sharon said. "Vicky is part of us and we need to locate her."

"Yes. I'm part of the group, now that Sharon and I are together. I'll do anything to help. I'll take Judy's part since she isn't here."

"New thoughts. New ideas. New person who also cares," I said. "It sounds like an unbeatable force."

"Agreed."

We drank the wine, ate the meal with a lively discussion about the weather and the story about Judy falling down near the Home. It ended in laughter.

"Nancy, have you heard if she's home?" Sharon asked.

"Not yet. She should be soon. I hope she'll message or text us."

When finished with the meal, we cleared the table and I placed the food in containers and put them into the refrigerator. Peggy wanted to load the dishwasher, but I told her it could wait.

"Do you want us around the table?" I asked.

"That would be great."

Will went for the small box and brought it to the dining room where us three were already seated and waiting for him.

I was on his right and Sharon his left with Peggy beside her on the other side.

"Let's see your little boy stash," Sharon said.

"This cigar box had once belonged to my dad. He loved to smoke them on Sunday afternoons. His 'stogie,' he'd call it." Will opened the lid. "It's not much, really."

"Let us be the judge," I said.

"Let's begin with my squirt gun."

"Tell us about it. Had you brought it to the Home?"

"Do the police know about it?"

"My gosh! Let him speak," I said.

"It's like this—everything in here I'd had from before Vicky left us. This fingernail, you see," he pointed to it, "that broke off when she was trying to zip her dress for the prom. It landed on the floor and for some reason, I picked it up." Frowning, he looked at each of us. "It was as if I had a premonition or something that I should save everything of my sister's."

"Do the police know about any of these items?" I asked. "They must know about the yo-yo and marbles? Nowadays, the police dig a lot deeper and take so much for evidence, if they think it may be relevant."

"I doubt they know about my stash." He shook his head. "Way back in 1970? They didn't collect much for evidence. There was no DNA testing, either."

"That's true. Crime scenes are treated differently nowadays," I said.

"What about the squirt gun? Did you have it at the Home? Anyone else touch it?" Sharon asked.

"If you set it down, any patient could've picked it up and tried it out," Peggy said.

"Let me think about this a minute," Will said. He began placing the items back into the box.

"We should put the nail in a plastic bag," I said. "I'll get you one. We only want your prints on these things."

"That's true," Sharon said.

"You must read a lot of mysteries?" Peggy said.

"I do. I like to shiver and shake at night." I grinned as I pulled out a small bag to use. I handed it over to Will who placed it in the bag.

"Thanks. Do you think I should take this box and everything inside to the police station?"

"Yes, most definitely," Sharon said, nodding.

"Go to the southside precinct, right where it all started. We saw a Detective Johnson. Walk right in and tell them who you are," I said, then remembered, "I do have his number and card. Hold on."

When I returned with the card, both Peggy and Sharon were yawning.

"Busy day tomorrow?"

"Yes. I have a funeral in the morning and a celebration of life in the evening. Two elderly parishioners died. It's a dirty shame. They were both widowed and very sweet."

"How sad," Will said. "We never know when our time's up, do we?"

"That we don't," Sharon said. She got up from the table and looked at me. "Next week, Nancy, after I meet with the bishop, we'll get together. It'll be at my house."

"You'll call?" I followed them to the hall closet.

"Yes." Sharon and Peggy started putting on their coats to leave.

"Okay, I'm looking forward to it." I gave her a hug. "Thank you."

"We'll keep each other informed about Judy and the search for Vicky?"

"Of course. Sharon, we're together forever. We've

been friends for decades and always will be." I turned to Peggy and hugged her also. "Thanks for coming."

"It was great to meet you Peggy and see you again, Sharon," Will said. He moved his full box into the living room and set it on the coffee table. He sat on the couch. When they'd left, he continued, "Have you heard from the park ranger or from the police since you went there?

"They have the diaries and are investigating further."

"Coffee? Tea?"

"I'm fine. Really, I can't stay much longer, but since Mother started talking about Vicky again, I feel like I need to find her. For some odd reason, I think Mom is hanging on to life until she has closure for Vicky."

"I think it sounds pretty normal. I wouldn't want to die either not knowing what happened to a child of mine. Think of the Wetterling family from the St. Cloud area. Jacob Wetterling was abducted and murdered October 11, 1989. His body wasn't found until 30 years later. Now they finally have closure after all of these years."

"I feel better knowing I'm trying to locate my sister. It's not as if I haven't thought about her over the years or looked for her in many strangers who have similar features. Sometimes I wonder if this isn't why my marriage didn't work? I wasn't able to give of myself for fear of abandonment."

"Don't feel alone with that one. I fell in love in my senior year and became engaged with a man who was sent to Vietnam. When Mike returned he broke our engagement. He was Sharon's brother and now deceased. He's the man found frozen outside of the veterans facility. I don't know much else." I glanced away, then back. "I never knew why he broke the engagement. That's what has always perplexed me because I knew he still loved me. He couldn't say that he didn't. Sharon has never revealed what she knows about it. I think she might in a few days. It'll be a release."

"I take it you were married and weren't able to find happiness because of it?"

"Yes, but I felt a load lifting from my shoulders the other day when the three of us could openly talk about the past. Judy later questioned the Agent Orange, and it may well have factored into his health issues."

"We understand each other." Will peered down at the box. "I think my life is about to change, but it'll be hard to go forward."

"I'm in agreement. To seek the truth for unanswered questions and fears will release us to enjoy our life. The next stage, if you will, or act."

"I believe it's act three." He stood up and said, "I know what I must do and will take care of it before work. Thanks for listening."

"Thanks to you, too. I've needed someone to listen to me for years. There are too many people who think they know more about me than I know."

"I have a feeling that the past is going to—"

"Run right over us."

From the window I watched as his headlights

became meshed with shadows.

I shut the lights off and sat in darkness, letting my thoughts of Mike circle around and around to the sweet memories stored inside.

And wept for my life that never was.

Judy
Chapter Seventeen

The drive home seemed short because I slept most of the way. We stopped for a light meal midway, and Carl brought me home and stayed for an hour or a little longer. He made sure I was settled for the night before leaving.

Needless to say, I was exhausted. The word tired and completely exhausted would've defined me. The time with Nancy and Sharon was fabulous but since I wasn't at home, I hadn't been able to care properly for myself. I came to the conclusion my well-being must come first. Most of all, I wanted to feel loved and wanted. In many ways, I was able to see the future if I stayed on this path.

I had loved being with Carl and loved the manner in which he cared for me. Why did I go so wrong so many years ago? My circle of life was broken. The crack from not having my girlfriends near added another fracture. It was time to make not just me whole again but everyone else within the fold of love and friendship, but it wasn't just on my shoulders. We all had to want it.

Once my head hit the pillow, I slept until late morning. It was so nice to have my own comfort. One of the first chores of the morning was to make coffee and find something decent to eat. As I went about my duties, it was apparent Carl had spent time going through my cupboards and cabinets and emptying all of my liquor bottles. The garbage bag was overflowing. Evidently, he wanted me to see what he'd done and that he'd be looking out for my welfare or should I say, "addiction"? I was glad. It was time I was treated like a child because I'd behaved like one for too many years. After I had my coffee and fried an egg, I went for my phone.

The first person on my list to call was Carl.

"Good morning."

"You too. How do you feel?"

"Ragged and tired, but good. Thanks for everything, Carl. You're a dear."

"You're my dear and I want it to stay that way."

"Me too," I said. "I'm making the relevant phone calls once we disconnect."

"Good and keep me informed. If you need a chauffer, I'm your man."

"Thanks."

We disconnected and I began calling the numbers on my list.

I called my insurance agent.

My car, of course, was totaled and my license suspended. I looked down at my feet and said, "You're it. My new wheels."

Next I called the attorney, the person Carl recommended.

"Hello," I said. I held my breath, and my heart pounded. "May I please speak to Summer Paisley?

This is in regards to my driving status and recent out of state accident." I gave the receptionist my name and poured another cup of coffee as I waited for an answer.

"Summer Paisley." I heard a faint sympathetic note in her voice. "Tell me about you."

I went ahead and relayed all the needed information so she could locate the information on file and also told her about my teaching job at the university.

"You're not going to like it. Want to come in for an office visit or get the news over the phone?" She waited a minute, then said, "I've had many clients in the same predicament over the years, and you're not going to like what I have to say."

"That bad?" I took a moment and said, "Well…what is it?" I gripped the phone tightly. "I already know the charges and that I can't drive, so tell me something new." I held my breath.

"We're talking jail time," Summer said.

"Jail?" I was sunk and knew it. It felt as if my heart dropped to my knees. "I'll lose my job."

"You get yourself checked in for treatment somewhere, and do it now."

"Geez."

As soon as we disconnected, I stared at the wall in front of me.

I contacted my doctor who made the formal arrangements for admittance into a treatment center.

I didn't like it but knew it had to be done. I was ready to admit I was a drunk.

Before Carl was contacted, I walked to the neighborhood grocery store and picked myself up a carton of cigarettes, chocolate ice cream, a dozen chocolate covered donuts, a loaf of bread, eggs, and a couple cans of soup. That was the limit of what these old bones and muscles could carry, I found out as I trudged home.

Magdalene called from work shortly after the groceries were put away.

"Judy? Are you being admitted for treatment?"

"I'm waiting for a call from the doctor but it looks like I'll be admitted soon, but the dates aren't set. My car, of course, is totaled. I know the insurance rates will be beyond my paycheck for quite a while. My license is suspended."

"What are your plans after treatment. Are you returning to work or retiring?"

"I don't have a definite answer," I said. "I'll let you know by the end of the quarter. How is the student assistant doing?"

"We're doing double time all around the department because of you, missy."

"I don't like my situation anymore than you do."

"When you have definite dates, call and let me know so the students aren't without a teacher."

"Yes, I will."

She disconnected before I could say, "boo," which was fine by me. She was always a crochety old biddy.

I lit a smoke, rinsed an ashtray, refilled my coffee cup, and took all of it out to sit in the living room to relax. Magdalene had shattered my spirit. All I could think of was having a drink. A really good, stiff bump of whiskey.

Maybe retiring was the way to go? Did I really like teaching?

My phone dinged alerting me to a message. It was from Sharon. *How are you?* I decided to send a group message with Sharon and Nancy. *I'm okay. Kind of down right now. I slept like a log last night. The verdict is treatment or jail. I'm more than ready to accept my addictions and admit that I can't go it alone. We need each other. Thanks.*

Sharon responded: *Good. Stay in touch and check your email.*

Nancy messaged: *Keep us in the know. I'll also pray for you and for us. Will is bringing a box of his childhood memories to the detective this morning. I'll send a message when I learn more. Have a good day.*

Good day to everyone.

I really didn't know what to think. Then there was Nancy. Trustworthy, loyal, and honest—Nancy. She was the most dependable. Sharon's email spoke of all the hurt, pain, and suffering I had lived through. How she knew my parents treated me badly, and she always felt a pang in her heart for me. Her hope was for me to return to church. To pray. She said the power of prayer was heavenly, and she'd added my name on a prayer list. I'd be prayed for at every Tuesday prayer group as well as Sunday worship service.

Through blurry eyes, I turned on the TV and searched for *Murder She Wrote*. I loved Angela Lansbury. At the end of the episode, the doctor's office called. I would be able to check in at the treatment center in the morning, and I'd be an inpatient there for two weeks. Eight o'clock. He also said it was time for this to happen, and he would support me in any way possible. I thanked him for that before saying, "Goodbye."

I gave Carl a phone call, leaving him a voice message. Magdalene answered on the second ring, and she was pleased it happened so quickly. I was too. Then, I sent a message to the two and sat back to relax.

More bricks lifted from my shoulders. I wanted to celebrate. How did non-addicted people celebrate? What did they do if they didn't drink? Go binge shopping? I wondered as I stared at the TV. I went and retrieved the quart of newly purchased ice cream and watched one show after another while I ate it. By the time it was almost gone, my stomach was making funny noises.

My energy picked up, and I washed the clothes plus vacuumed and cleaned the bathrooms. When finished, I decided what clothes to pack and hoped I had enough underpants to wear without having to wash them.

Carl sent me a message stating he'd be over with supper and to spend the night. He wanted to take me to the center because he didn't want me to go alone.

His message brought tears to my eyes. *How could I have let him go*? By the time the table was set and the suitcase near the door, Carl arrived with chicken chow mein, my favorite.

"You're wonderful," I said.

"Thanks. You're brave and courageous, Judy."

"Thanks. Please continue holding my hand."

"You have the strength to make it. You must do it for you."

"I know, but thank you for your support and confidence."

We finished our meal. Carl called dibs on the spare room. When I asked him why not spend the night in my bed, he replied the time wasn't right. I realized as I closed my eyes, he was right. I wasn't ready yet for our relationship to blossom once again. The newly purchased set of panties and bra would have to wait for another time.

Morning came none too soon. I'd tossed and turned most of the night. At six, I was up and showering, dressed by seven. Carl was right behind me. We silently drank our coffee like it was a day of doom, then all of sudden, the sun shone right in my eyes.

"I think I'm getting a message from Sharon or God. Not sure which one."

"What makes you say that?"

"The sun is blinding me. It's time for me to see and smell the roses and enjoy the new day." I smiled. "Let's go."

"That's what I needed to hear."

Carl made sure the house was secure before we walked out into the sunshine and crisp morning air. He held my hand as we walked into the center. Once inside, I was quickly taken to my room with barely enough time to say, "Thanks."

The day slid past with a morning session where I was introduced and forced to say why I was there. I also had to talk a little bit about myself. That was the hard part. If I spoke too much about me, then I had little to hide.

The room was small and the dresser barely large enough to hold my belongings. A laundry basket sat in the corner.

I hated the meals. They tasted like cardboard. No flavor. I hated the people surrounding me at my assigned table. No manners. Grunting. Gobbling. Using fingers when a fork was in order, or not using a napkin.

At least my parents had taught me decent table manners. *Chalk up one good attribute learned from childhood.*

When the call for lights off came, I clicked the button and rolled over.

No smoking in the rooms, either, which bugged me big time.

The hard bed didn't give much comfort, but eventually I slept. I woke to rapping on the door. "Just a minute!" I slipped into my robe and tied the belt.

"Time to get up," the nurse said. She rapped again.

"All set," I said. I opened the door. "Morning."

"You, too." She handed over a cup with a blood pressure pill.

"Thanks." I swallowed it with the given water. "I'll dress and be right down to breakfast."

"Sure thing. It's a choice of all three, pancakes, bacon, or cereal."

I watched her leave and shut the door. Oh, how I ached for my kitchen chair, counter, coffee cup, and toaster. I missed my refrigerator filled with junk. No fresh veggies. I must change my diet, I promised myself. My way of life, too.

Yesterday's clothes lay on top of the laundry basket. I pulled open the dresser drawer, removing my black pants and red sweater set. I brushed out my hair, washed my face, brushed my teeth, and headed from the room into the hallway.

My lungs felt better without the early morning smoke. I should give them up, but one thing at a time. I'd already promised myself to give up drugs and alcohol.

As I eyed the residents surrounding the dining room tables and those in line, I thought how lucky I was I still had teeth. So many didn't.

The counselors encouraged making new friends and having conversations during meal time. They patrolled in the background.

"Is it good?" I asked. The person next to me never spoke or if he did, it was slow. I wanted to wind him up. My nickname for him was Dynamite.

"Hm," Dynamite muttered.

Big talker, here.

To my other side, I said, "Gladys. How's the cakes?"

"It's not my birthday," Gladys said.

"I'll keep that in mind," I said. I dug into my pancakes after pouring maple syrup across the top of the stack. To the people sitting opposite, I said,

"How's the grains?" They had cereal.

"Not bad," one said. "Stan's not my name."

"Okay," I replied.

So much for conversation, I thought as I sliced my pancakes and devoured them. When finished, it was group time. We each had assigned rooms. Dynamite and I were lucky, it was right down the hall. We walked together.

"Come in and find a chair," Dick said upon entry. He stood tall with slicked back black hair. "We're short two people." He had glasses and a straight, pert nose. Today he wore a blue plaid shirt. Yesterday's shirt was a light blue. The man's imagination took a U-turn after second grade.

"What happened to them?" I asked.

"Discharged. It may be just the three of us." Dick grinned. "It'll be nice for us to chat about ourselves."

Inwardly, I groaned. The last thing I wanted was to talk about myself, and Dick knew it because of yesterday's session. I liked listening to stories, not telling them. Why couldn't Dynamite be released instead of the girls who were discharged?

"Just what I'm looking forward to," I said, "a nice, intimate session." I meant it as sarcastically as it sounded.

"I'll try and do better," Dynamite said.

"Won't that be nice?" Thank heavens he picked up on that.

"Let's get started," Dick said.

"Okay, if you insist," I said. "Where should we begin?"

"Let's talk about your families," Dick said. "We'll start with you, Judy."

I rolled my eyes and groaned. This was going to be a very long hour. I prayed for deliverance but knew that wouldn't happen. Why couldn't there be a tornado drill like in the public schools?

"My parents drank. They beat each other up. Both worked. Mother was hard on me. Yes, I've forgiven her. No money. End of story." I crossed my arms. "Now, I've nothing more to say on the subject."

Dick's eyebrows twitched. "That's good for now." Nodding to Dynamite, he said, "Your turn."

"I, ah, I, well—I'm not sure, you know. Don't really know what to, ah, say, really." He shrugged. "You know how it is? My mom, well? I'm not sure. She, ah, well, she," Dynamite said. He scratched his greasy hair. "She, ah, left us kids when I was two." He shrugged. "Don't, ah, know—you see? Not much else to say, ah, about her, now is there?"

Dick glanced from one to another. *Now he'll ask about Dad.*

"This is a great beginning," Dick said. He looked at me, then at Dynamite. "How about your dad or father figure?"

I knew it! I should bet against myself to see who'd win!

"Father figure?" Dynamite said. His brows arched. "Oh, I get it." He hesitated before continuing. "He, ah—"

"Your biological father."

I wish Dynamite would speak. Just answer him.

"What?" Dynamite asked. He scratched his hair.

"Your father? Did he marry your mother? Your real dad?"

I want my room. I want to be away from these people. I want to be home. Patience, Judy. Patience is the key thread you're lacking.

"The man who raised me wasn't my real dad." Dynamite pulled his whiskers. "It's, ah, it's kinda hard to talk about, you see?"

"I think I should get a pair of pliers and extract all the info you need from him. I'll be right back," I said. I stood and went to the door. "I'll see you later. Have a good one."

"This will be on your record," Dick said.

"Bite me."

Nancy
Chapter Eighteen

The weather had changed overnight. Snow clouds loomed overhead, threatening. The forecast didn't sound good—a winter storm brewed in the west and would soon pass through town.

Will had called early morning and asked if I would meet him at the police station because he thought I could bolster his confidence when he spoke with the detective.

I drove to a drive-thru and purchased a cup of coffee and a roll. The early morning traffic made me realize how much I enjoyed retirement. The drive took longer than normal, but finally I parked and hurried indoors.

"Will!" I shivered. "Brrr!"

"The weather switched overnight."

"I'm glad Judy left when she did. It would've been miserable had she extended her stay to today." I unbuttoned my coat. "Have you given them your name?"

"Yes, and the detective will be out shortly," he said. Will picked up the box with the items he planned to give to the detective. "I hope these will help. I want Mom to have closure."

"You need it too."

"Yes, you're right."

At that very moment, the detective opened the door.

"Hello. Detective Johnson here for Mr. Storbaekkene and Nancy Bjork. Correct?"

"Yes."

"Follow me, please. We'll talk and take a look at what you have."

We walked with him to his office.

"Have a seat."

Will took the one nearest to the desk and placed the box atop of it.

"I remember you, and I'm still very sad about not being able to find your sister," Detective Johnson said. "It's always tough, but let's see what you have?" He reached for the box and opened it. "Tell me about the nail."

"It's Vicky's, and she'd cracked her nail when she was dressing for the prom." Will glanced out the window. "I remember thinking, what a different color nail polish. I took it for some odd reason. I am older than her, so why take it? It's the type of thing a little kid would take."

"If this has been handled or not stored properly, there won't be any DNA on it worth saving," Detective Johnson said. "We'll have to wait and see what the labs tell us."

"What else do you have of Vicky's?" I asked.

"We only found a necklace left behind of hers. That's it. It's the only piece of evidence we have that belonged to her. No fabric. Hair or anything found near the necklace." Detective Johnson looked at me, then Will. "Who placed the nail in the bag?"

"I was at Nancy's last night. Sharon was there and her friend. It was Nancy's idea."

"You touched it?"

"No." I shook my head. "I got the bag, and he placed it inside. No one touched any of the items last night."

"We need your fingerprints, both of you," Johnson said. "It'll help in the identification. Let's go ahead, Will, and get your DNA while we're at it."

"Sounds good."

We both nodded.

"The squirt gun?"

"I had it at the Soldier's Home a few times. Jackson took it from me once. When I was a kid, way back when."

Johnson placed it in an evidence bag and labeled it as well as the fingernail. "Next?"

"Marbles. I used to play with them when I'd visit my dad sometimes. I thought I'd bring them along. Never know what you guys might find interesting when you're investigating."

"What, if anything, did you find near those two stones?" I asked.

"Interesting question, Nancy." Johnson leaned back in his chair and folded his hands behind his head. "Nothing really, but there are a few little tidbits that have raised some red flags and caught our interest."

"That's good news, then. Right?" I said. "And the pictures? Diary?"

"Our forensic team are studying everything and will put together a report."

"Please keep me informed," Will said. "My mom seems to regress more often than ever into the past. She's always bringing up some such thing about Vicky. It's time to bring my baby sister home."

"We'll do our best," Johnson said. He stood. "We'll be in contact as soon as we've gone through all the evidence once again."

"Thank you." I stood and began to button my coat.

"Thank you." Will slid back his chair and shook hands with the detective. Hands were shaken all around.

Once we returned to the front waiting room, what I saw through the window made me cringe—snow.

"I have off from work until noon. There's just enough time for a quick cup of coffee. Interested?"

"You bet." I found the invitation thrilling. "Where to?"

"There's a coffee shop right around the corner."

"I'll follow. I'm parked right across the street."

"It looks like I'm parked near."

We hurried across to our receptive cars and jumped inside. After he slowed when he came near, I began to drive from the curb and let him lead the way. As I drove the short distance, my thoughts went to the meeting with Johnson. He wasn't very forthcoming with new clues or evidence. I'd hoped to learn more, especially about what Judy and I had discovered. I made a mental note to send a message to her and Sharon.

I wondered about Judy. Was she responding to treatment? I thought she might because of the way it sounded. To me, she seemed ready to face everything the psychologist asked of her. She was finally facing all of her secrets, not just the ones we knew about, but every last one of them, imagined or not. Also, dealing with her parents and the effects of alcohol couldn't be easy, either. My heart poured out to her, and I said a prayer in her honor as I parked beside Will in the nearby parking lot.

"What did you think of Johnson?" I asked of Will.

"Not sure."

We walked side-by-side until he stopped to open the door for me to enter with him following. It was a serve yourself type coffeehouse so I ordered my latte and he did the same. When the drinks were made, we carried them to an open table and had a seat.

"I think he knew more than what he said, but I understand why he didn't say more. My hopes of finding Vicky are rapidly skyrocketing. I can't think at work. I'm basically good for nothing."

"It's got to be miserable to have lived all these years without the knowledge of what happened to her. The basic—Where? When? And why?"

"My mom's having a hard time which is why she went to Margo's funeral." He sipped his coffee. "I'm glad you came for coffee with me. I'd like to know your take on all of this. Has Johnson hinted at any one particular thing of interest that you know of?"

"I honestly can't think of what it might be," I said. The coffee was hot and the aroma was heavenly. "It didn't seem like he knew anything about Jackson, but maybe he didn't want to say anything. They have to keep clues and thoughts to themselves, too, so as not to impede an investigation."

"Hmmm. I was asked about friends, boyfriends, where she hung out, work related questions. Everything was of that nature, never about Dad's work. He worked long hours and was never home, but that's how it was back then. Mom didn't work. She looked after us kids and took care of everything. Since the Home was near and he did maintenance, sometimes we could visit if he was outside mowing or having lunch. The staff didn't mind us coming in. It wasn't that type of a hospital where you had to stay away, it was a place for old soldiers to live. We had Civil War vets up until the last one died in 1956, I think, and vets from the other wars. These men needed someplace to live, so many were homeless and didn't fit into society once they'd returned from battle."

"It can't be any different than it is now. Look at the men and women suffering from lost limbs and the women being separated from their children. The horrible suicide bombers. It's terrible."

"I believe we're on the right track, and I'm grateful to Mom for having the gumption to resume the search."

"Me too."

We finished our coffee.

"I have to get going. Do you mind if I contact you again?"

"I'd love it. I think we've both needed a friend who will listen."

"And, for me, someone who loved my sister and wants her found almost as much as I do." He waited a beat then said, "I'll call if I hear anything at all from Johnson. How about dinner some evening?"

"I'd love it," I said and smiled.

We parted company, he in his car and me in mine. After starting the engine up, I thought of my mother. Mother always wanted me to remarry and have a family. She hated that there weren't any grandchildren. I think she hated me for it, too. Once Dad passed on, she grew distant and rather self-absorbed. I'd hear of her going out to eat with friends and enjoying evenings spent with them and their families, which only added to my chagrin. It dismayed me to know Mom enjoyed being with someone else's family and not with me. A very long time ago, I decided it was her way of punishment for not having grandchildren.

I wondered if Mom would know me when I saw her? I wanted to try to jiggle her memory about Vicky. Could she have some hidden knowledge? She might, but would she remember? And I wanted to let her know that I was interested in another man.

The nursing home was located on Highway 100, which was a bit of a drive from my current location but on the way home. Road conditions weren't the greatest but typical of Minnesota in the winter time, a little slippery. I gave the nursing home a call to let them know I would be arriving shortly. The last time,

I hadn't called and Mom was sleeping. I hadn't wanted to wake her. Mom was eighty-five years old.

Thirty minutes later, I parked near the main front entrance, shut the car off and walked inside the doors that brought me to the main desk.

"Hi. I just called saying I planned to visit Mabel Einerson. Is she ready for me?"

"Of course! She down the hall in the TV room. They're watching *I Love Lucy* reruns."

"Thanks."

I headed down the hallway toward the small room where I found her watching the show. Her eyes sparkled behind glasses, just how I remembered from childhood. *Will she remember me now?*

"Mom?" I said, kneeling before her. "Mom? This is Nancy."

"Nancy who?"

"Your daughter." Tears filled my eyes. *Will it always be like this?* "I have news for you."

"You don't look like Nancy," she said, squinching her eyebrows as she looked at me. "Nancy?"

"You don't have any other daughter." I hugged her. "Love you, Mom." Suddenly she sat straighter and looked me in the eye after I'd released my hold. "It's me, Nancy."

"Are you here to see me?"

"Yes. Can we go and talk privately somewhere?"

When she'd nodded her answer, I began to wheel her down the hallway toward her room.

"What do you want from me?" she said.

Once inside the room, I placed her near the

window and hoped the sunshine would improve her memory.

"Mom? Do you remember Vicky? You do remember her, don't you?"

I studied her as she searched her mind for an answer.

"Was that your friend?"

"Yes. The girl that went away after the high school prom."

"I'm not sure that I remember her." She frowned. "Did she play dolls and house with you?"

"Yes. There was me, Judy, Vicky, and Margo."

"Did your handsome Marine ever return home?"

"Mom. Focus on Vicky."

"No grandchildren. Why not? I wanted little ones to have around."

Frustrated, I sighed, ready to walk out the door.

"What did she look like?"

"Pretty with a wonderful smile."

My phone dinged a message as she sat quietly, staring out the window. I glanced at it.

"That girl. Her boyfriend did it. The smug look on his face when he was interviewed. His picture was on the news, remember? Beady eyes, he had. His hair was long and in a ponytail. What man wears ponytails? He was on drugs. That's who did it!"

"Thanks Mom for your impressions."

"Well, you asked. Now I've got my program to watch."

"Do you want to go back with your friends?"

"Yes."

She grumbled and mumbled the entire way to where she'd formerly been. I was happy to leave and get into my car. Before driving from the lot, I glanced at the earlier message. It read: *Judy's on suicide watch. I'm getting the updates. Carl.*

I responded: *I'll pray for her. Should I come?*

I also relayed the message to Sharon before I drove out of the parking lot.

The knowledge about Judy's suicide watch took my breath away. It felt as if Judy was barely treading water. Tears filled my eyes as I awaited Carl's response. Besides Carl, who else was on her side? She must not have close friends. This was why we absolutely had to remain in touch and close to each other. We all needed someone to be with us at a moment in need. Carl must really love her.

It wasn't a long wait before a response came from both.

Carl texted: *She's been opening up about her childhood. It sounds like her life crashed down on her shoulders. I'll keep you updated, but she's being well taken care of and I've taken a few days off from work to be with her. Prayers are good and the best thing to do for her. Carl.*

Sharon message: *I'm calling tonight about 7.*

I tried not to think about Mom on the long drive home. Once I entered 35W, I felt better. As I drove, my thoughts went to Judy. I wondered if she still read voraciously? She used to read Nancy Drew as a child. We'd exchange books all summer long.

When I stopped for gas, a strip mall was nearby. One of the stores had antiques, so I wandered over to it. I couldn't believe my find. An old Nancy Drew book was on the shelf for twenty dollars. The copyright was dated 1952. I bought it, knowing Judy would love it.

It took another half hour until I entered my garage and shut off the car before entering the house. I sent Carl a message requesting Judy's address.

The evening drifted past with me reliving that weekend and Judy's accident. Judy was never what you'd call sweet. She was always right on the mark with her snappy answers. She held you accountable. Didn't anyone hold her accountable? What about Carl? Was he still in love with her? Did she realize nothing that happened to her was her fault? Sometimes, your parents were your own worst enemies. They either parented too much or too little. The correct attention, discipline, or direction wasn't forthcoming. From being around children, I'd learned that some children needed to think and be alone while others needed plenty of direction.

Judy's temper flared easily. She was easily hurt and offended plus had trouble with authority. Few realized that in her because she often acted cavalier. I knew because her guard was down in my presence. Judy was slowly going down the rabbit hole. It was time for her to see the light once again.

Judy
Chapter Nineteen

Embarrassed is the word that came to mind when I realized what I had done to myself. I was better than this. I'd lived through hell and came out on the other side many times. Why had I tried to take my life? Facing all my failures and heartaches wasn't easy, but with Carl by my side, I knew I'd win. I was also positive that Nancy and Sharon were there for me also. I told myself to buck up and face the music. I sat straighter in my chair and took a deep breath. No way was I going to let Dick get the better of me with his questions, nor that dim-wit, Dynamite.

"Judy? How do you feel? Do you need anything?" Dick's voice was soft like butter. "If you need me at all, just press the button." He looked at me through the bars of my cell. Supposedly it was impossible to carry out a suicide mission in these small cells, but I'd heard of people doing it. *If you want to die – there's a will – there's a way.*

"I've made a mess of myself."

"Honey, we'll get you through this and you'll come out on the other side, healthy."

"I hope so." I gulped back tears.

"No—you will. You're a good person. You're smart, educated, have a great job, and you have friends who love you."

"I never knew until recently."

"You're a wonderful person and don't ever forget it," Dick said. "Are you ready to re-enter the world?" He studied me.

"I'm pretty sure I'm ready," I said. I looked him square in the eye. "This isn't easy."

"I'm sure it isn't," Dick said. "Nothing is nowadays."

"Got that right," I said. "I'm not sure what to say."

"I think we should leave you for a few more hours. It'll give you needed time to rest and continue with your soul-searching."

"Soul-searching? That's what this journey is called?"

"It's an expression," Dick said. "If you need anything, an attendant is right outside. I'll come asap."

"Thanks."

I wasn't sure what to think. Dick didn't quite seem like he had his eye on the ball, but maybe working with suicidal maniacs 24/7 will do that to you. Then there was Dynamite. I wondered if he wasn't the person who drove me to this suicidal state? That man drove me nuts. What was it Mom always lectured me about? *Patience.* That was what it was. I needed to learn patience. Well, being in this situation would be a learning curve for me.

An attendant came for me at four o'clock for a meeting with Dick.

"You look good," Dick said. He nodded toward the chairs. "Have a seat."

"Okay." I sat in the nearest of the two.

"Carl is very worried about you," Dick said. "He seems very kind and cares deeply for you."

"We were married once. I blew it because of my habits." I sat farther back, knowing it was turning into a question and answer meeting. "He's thoughtful."

"He's mentioned your friends, Nancy and Sharon, and that they send their love and prayers."

"Nancy the love part, Sharon the prayers bit."

"Are they close friends?"

"Yes, childhood. Actually, Nancy from grade school. Sharon, high school and is now a minister."

"Do you think she's the opposite of yourself?"

"What do you mean?" That question caught me off guard. "She has a congregation and is gay. She has an appointment with the bishop to reveal her sexual preference, and then she'll inform the parish. I don't envy her, not one bit."

"What happened with your marriage?" Dick asked. "You've admitted to drugs and alcohol. Is that all?"

"What are you getting at?" I asked. Staring over his shoulder at the framed diploma, I ignored him.

"You're not going to get by easily," Dick said. "Tell me what's eating you. What caused you to sneak a knife into your room and try slitting your wrist? What's deep inside?"

"My life has always been dreadful. Nothing ever changes." I glanced away.

"You're not making this any easier, and you're not going to be transferred from suicide watch until you face yourself head-on."

"What do you want from me? You want me to admit I'm a failure? That's it, isn't it? I'm a failure! A-1!" I said. "Are you happy? I've admitted it! A-1—good for nothing bum!" I curled my fists. "Can I go now? Are you satisfied?" I slammed my fist down.

"Hold on a minute here," Dick said. He leaned forward in his chair and eyed me closely. "That's not all. Why do you feel like this?"

"Could it be because my parents were awful? Is it because I was drugged at a party back in 1970? Do you think that might be it?"

"Now we're getting somewhere," Dick said. "Tell me about the party."

"It was after graduation. Parties everywhere," I said and continued with the story, ending with, The nightmare became vivid, and I reached for more tissues to wipe my tears. "It continued forever."

"What happened afterward?"

"I must've passed out. I don't know how long I lay there."

"Alone?"

"Yes, but I heard voices outside the door. I glanced outside, and the sun was rising. I gathered my wits and hobbled out the door."

"What did you do next?"

"Went home." I shook my head.

"You've kept it in this long?"

"I didn't tell anyone. I tried to push it from my mind."

"Did that help?"

"No." I shook my head.

"Why not?"

"I'm filled with guilt."

"It's not your fault. I want you to say that."

"It's not my fault," I softly said.

"Say it with meaning."

"It's not my fault!"

"Once more."

"It's *not* my fault!" *I feel dizzy.*

"Just what was needed," Dick said. "Take in a few long breaths and tell me how you feel."

"Better," I said. I took a couple more breaths. "I feel lighter."

"We'll talk more in the morning. You've had a very huge breakthrough."

"I feel relieved."

"That's just what I wanted to hear," Dick said. Leaning back, he smiled. He pressed a button and said, "I'll walk Judy back to her room."

I stood and blew my nose again.

The following day, I was allowed to receive messages. Nancy notified me that a package was in the mail and that I'd love the present. I hoped it wasn't bunny pajamas.

I felt shaky or rocky and scared I might reach for the bottle once released. As I worked on focusing and pulling myself together, I realized how lucky I was to be alive and on the road to recovery. Finally, I was beginning to feel comfortable in my own skin. My room consisted of a single bed, small dresser, and small bathroom. I wasn't allowed toiletry items except my toothbrush and toothpaste. All medicine was administered by the medical staff.

Two days later, the package was received. Inside was a Nancy Drew book. *The Case of the Hidden Clock.* It had been my favorite. I read it from cover to cover and smiled at the end.

The night before my release, I went to my room and read Sharon's message once again and smiled.

I was beloved from friends and my former husband—my best friend.

It felt terrific.

Nancy
Chapter Twenty

I had been called to teach once again but declined. My heart wasn't in it anymore. Knowing Judy was having such difficulty really was bothersome. Sharon planned to tell the bishop today about her orientation. I said a silent prayer to give both strength. I hadn't wanted to leave the house either for fear of being needed by Sharon or Judy. Or what if Detective Johnson had a few more questions or Will wished to speak to me? I had to be home.

As the day wore on, I busied myself instead reading, searching the internet for Christmas presents, and worrying about my friends. My phone buzzed mid-afternoon and it was Judy. At last!

"Nancy! I can't thank you enough for the book. Whatever made you think of it or remember that it had been one of my favorites? The next question is, where on earth did you ever find it? EBay?"

"I had gone to visit my mother and when I stopped for gas, there was an antique store nearby. The book was on a shelf, staring at me."

"Well, thank you. That was very kind."

"You're welcome."

"This is one of the nicest gifts I've received."

"Good. I'm glad you like it."

"Actually we could swap books, couldn't we?"

"Most likely." I fanned myself. "These hot flashes are enough to make me want to put my head in the freezer. How about you?"

"I agree. Sometimes, I think I'm going to blow up," Judy said. "Just as fast as they show up and annoy me, they leave. Doctors really don't know much about them, either."

"Carl notified me."

"That was good of him," Judy said. "My time is up. I'm only allowed a few minutes and the phone Nazi is staring and wagging his finger at me."

"It's good to hear you're doing so well. Call me again, Judy. I love you."

"I love you too. Hugs and kisses."

"Yes. X's and O's."

I sat down with a cup of tea and a plate of leftover roast and vegetables from the night before and ate my evening meal. Sometimes it felt lonesome sitting and eating. Other times, I was happy alone. Tonight, I wished for company. Will came to mind. I honestly wondered about him. Did he blame himself for his sisters' abduction? I knew little of him except being Vicky's older brother. I did believe he had children but didn't know.

My life would've been so different had Mike married me. We would've had children. Children. My heart skipped a beat. I'd wanted children with him in the worst way.

I continued eating, finishing with a large dish of vanilla ice cream.

With reruns of *Cheers* in the background, I picked up my computer and began a search on Jackson Gunderson. First off, I typed in Vicky's name and discovered newspapers reports and vital statics. I deeply sighed and wondered if she'd ever be found. It also caused me to wonder what she'd look like today? Would she have had children? Married Steve Turner? Gosh, I wished I'd helped in the search so much more than what I had. It seemed like yesterday even though I knew it was forty-eight years ago. We carried on with our lives and now I was searching for her online. Time had radically changed our methods of staying in touch.

Jackson's name popped up in a cemetery near Fergus Falls. The record of his time at the Soldier's Home, also. It proved he was a patient since he disappeared the day of the abduction. The geography surrounding the Home showed the falls, all the woods and parking plus the open land for visitors. Next, I went ahead and tried to track down relatives of his and found another Gunderson. It made me wonder if there were relatives of Jackson's in the town? I had to know.

I gave Sharon a call.

"Sharon? It's me."

"How are you doing?"

"Fine. I've been researching online for Jackson. I believe he's buried in Fergus Falls. There used to be a Gunderson gas station and I wonder if Jackson had owned it?"

"That's a stretch," Sharon said. "Anything else?"

"I accompanied Will to the police station this morning where he turned over the box and the items he'd kept inside. We had coffee afterward, and I've discovered I do like him. Then I went to visit my mom who was in outer space, however, she believes that Steve Turner abducted her."

"I'm not going to be able to rest during my retirement until that girl is found."

"Me, neither."

"The bishop called and moved the appointment to tomorrow, and I will inform him of my decision to retire."

"What about telling him about you?"

"It won't be necessary."

"Yes it is. No hiding anymore."

"My appointment is at 9:00."

"How about going to Fergus afterward?"

"Great."

"I'll pick you up at ten."

We disconnected, and I made myself ready for bed.

As I crawled under the covers, I thought of the day ahead.

My iPad was nearby so I streamed easy listening jazz to assist me falling asleep. My mind went in circles with thoughts of Sharon and how it would go with the bishop. If she didn't expose her sexuality preference, how would that affect her? Wouldn't that mean she was giving in to society? I hoped she told him so then her conscience would be clear. I loved her dearly and wished we could've been sisters.

The final thoughts to flow through my mind before sleep befell me were about Vicky. I wondered what really became of her?

I woke to a bit of sunshine. Clouds still covered the sky, but it wasn't snowing. No snow on the roads meant a great day for a drive.

The morning hours filled with breakfast and readying myself for the drive ahead. I made sure there was an extra blanket in the car and two water bottles in case of poor road conditions. And, my warm boots should the need arise to walk to a station because of a flat tire and no phone connections because of bad weather or dead space.

When I was all set, with my warm, heavy Norwegian knitted sweater and purse, I went out to the car. Traffic was light as I entered the main thoroughfare and stopped for a coffee to go at the nearest drive-thru coffee shop.

Sharon sent a text as I drove onto the road saying that she'd be home in ten minutes. At a light, I sent an emoji, of a thumb's up. It took another twenty minutes before I drove into her driveway and stopped. She stood near the window and saw me, immediately walking to the car and climbing inside.

"It's good to see you," I said. We leaned into each other for a hug and kiss. "Tell me how it went?"

"Great! I'll be officially retired within the next three months. Another minister will take my place. Just like that. He took my resignation gracefully and when I relayed to him my sexual preference, he didn't say a thing. I feel good."

"As you should. That was terrific. I wondered if you'd tell him. Last night, it didn't sound as if you would."

"Oh, I knew I would. It took me a few days to muster up the nerve and to find the right words, but I was ready. Now Peggy and I can have an open, honest life together."

I drove from the neighborhood and headed toward Cedar Lake Street where the entrance for 94W was located. In a few minutes we were driving northwest. Fergus Falls was approximately a two hour drive through small farms, lakes, and plenty of good honest folks trying to eke out a living by their own grit and hard work.

"I didn't look any further for Jackson on the internet. I was surprised when his name popped up with an address in Fergus Falls. Or should I say, a cemetery plot? That's it. I never bothered to check further. He must be dead."

"Today may end up being great or a let down. Let me see if something else should pop up. What search engine did you use?"

"Google."

"Let me try Safari."

As we passed through the heart of Minneapolis, I was relieved to find the roads not too wet and driving relatively easy. Fewer cars were on the road the farther out of town we drove.

"Bingo!" Sharon said. "Listen to this."

Bradley Gunderson, convicted of killing his father Jackson Gunderson, former owner of Gunderson Gas

Station, has been given a second chance. His attorney worked hard and was able to drop the sentence. He will be paroled in six weeks.

"Wow!" I said. "What's the date of the article?"

"It's June, 1985. That means Bradley was a juvenile. The sentencing was likely different since if he wasn't an adult." Sharon continued, "I assume Bradley killed his father in December, 1983. He would've been twelve at the time. That would've made him about the right age, wouldn't it? If Vicky was abducted, and we have to assume she was raped, then this Bradley would've been twelve."

"The dates all fit, eh? But, is Bradley Vicky's son?"

"Good question. We're speculating."

"We're opening Pandora's Box."

"Most definitely."

We looked at the picked cornfields as we passed by the harvested land. It was a beautiful day.

"Should we eat first or do the cemetery?" I said.

"Let's go eat. I'm afraid once we see his final resting place, we may end up with horrible memories and won't feel like eating."

"Good point."

I took the 210 exit, which brought me into the heart of town. A small town diner stood on the corner of a block where I believed the gas station once stood, and I parallel parked in front of it.

"Impressive," Sharon said. She opened her car door and climbed out.

"Thanks." I climbed out also after shutting off the engine. "It's warmed up. The snow seems to be melting."

"Good!"

We sat beside a window and within a few minutes, we'd placed our orders of sandwiches and cups of homemade chicken soup. I got up to stroll around. Old pictures adorned the walls, and they called to me. I had to look at them. A picture from 1910 showed how Main Street looked. It was amazing how time changed everything. Another photo showed a man driving a horse and buggy into town with a woman beside him. I presumed it to be his wife. Farther along was a photo that really caught my eye. I waved Sharon over.

"Take a look at that picture. The man resembles Jackson."

"The year isn't recorded like the other pictures. I never met Jackson," Sharon said. "Do you think it's him?"

The waitress brought our meals to the booth and we went to sit down and eat.

"Well?" Sharon said.

"I think it is."

We ate our meal and afterward took a look at the pies in the counter. Sharon ordered a pumpkin and I requested an apple pie. We could tell by looking at them the crust was homemade. I was certain it would taste heavenly.

The meal was wonderful and the pie tasted divine, both of us thought so. We vowed to make a recommendation on line or give it a five-star if they had a website or Facebook page.

"I'm going for my last look at it and then pay the

bill. It's my treat because you drove."

Before I could protest, she was by the counter and paying. I placed a couple one dollar bills down for the tip, then got up to use the restroom. Upon my return, Sharon stood speaking with an older man who sat below the picture in a booth.

"The man in the picture reminds me of someone I once knew," I said, staring at it for a moment. "Do you happen to know who it is?"

"He was killed by his boy many a year ago." The man flipped his cap back and thought a minute. "He used to own the gas station."

"Gunderson?"

"Sounds right," he said.

"Any kids?"

"A boy. Good kid. The boy killed him when he was on another one of drunken rages. Bradley was the boy's name. Always wondered what happened to him."

"Where'd they live?" I asked.

"Way out in the country," he said. "East of town. First one that's totally abandoned. No one wanted the property. There's a condemned sign out front."

"Thanks," we both said.

"You done with me now?"

"You betcha!"

We went back to retrieve our coats and go to the cemetery.

Judy
Chapter Twenty-one

It was the middle of my final week at the clinic. The two weeks had gone by quickly. I was able to let-it-all-hangout, as they used to say in the sixties, and felt the better for doing so. All this stuff with my parents had been bottled up inside. I'd blamed myself for their drinking and cruelty. Shame on me. I knew it wasn't my fault they drank, which was why I drank. Forgetting the past and all the bad memories had been on my agenda, but not anymore. The party was past and gone, now I was fully exposed. And open. That was a good way to be. No more secrets. However, I was afraid, *afraid*, to tell Carl I still loved him. Afraid? Maybe I'd put it off until I was out of this joint.

But, what if he rejected me? I needed to be where I was safe and wouldn't reach for a bottle to hide my hurt and pain.

I had requested a different outfit to wear for this evening's dinner. It was going to be just Carl and me in my room. The door was able to remain closed for an hour's worth of privacy. I couldn't wait. Carl was to arrive in thirty minutes and I'd been dressed for an hour in a new skirt, sweater and scarf. No accessories.

Finally a folding table and two chairs were brought in and set up. An attendant pushed in a cart with the dishes and plasticware plus drinking glasses. It was all pretty. The design was of spring flowers. I loved it.

I paced the room for the next ten minutes. I thought for sure Carl would've arrived by now. *Didn't he say he'd be here early? He always was. He wouldn't have backed out, would he?*

Tears were on the verge of spilling from my eyes when I heard the familiar tip-tap of his shoes across the tile floor. He was here. I wiped my eyes and smiled.

"You look marvelous," I said. "You're just as handsome as ever."

"You, my dear, are beautiful," Carl said. He leaned over and kissed my cheeks. "I've got some great news."

"First, I have something to tell you." I breathed in deeply a few times. "I love you, Carl, and always have. I'm ready, if you are."

"That's music to my ears," Carl said. "I love you too, but we're going to take it slow."

"You're right. I'm always in a rush. How slow?"

"How about a few dates?"

"How about we move in together?"

"I don't want to be a crutch."

"You won't be."

"Let me think on it."

Just then, our meal of spaghetti and meatballs arrived with a crisp lettuce salad and dressing and garlic toasted bread.

We sat, staring into each other's eyes for a few minutes before we lifted the cover from our plate.

"I don't know if I've ever tasted anything so good before," I said. I took another bite and sipped from my glass filled with ice water. "It's delicious."

"I agree."

Carl was too polite to inform me that the reason behind the wonderful, delicious tasting food was that my tastebuds weren't corroded from drink. I felt like a kid again being beside him. The time was lovely.

"Have you heard from Judy or Sharon?" I wondered because of the horrible suicide attempt from a few days ago. I hadn't wanted them anymore concerned for my well-being.

"I've got news to tell you about Vicky."

"Really? Spit it out! Is she found? I bet she is. She's someplace in Norway, right?"

"Norway?"

"She took Norwegian in high school."

"Oh dear God. You took German. Well—I never knew."

"Yes, and Nancy took Norwegian, Margo—German. Now you know where our hearts lie." I thought for a minute. "Do you think she escaped and went to Norway? Who would know? It's possible, isn't it?"

"Slow down, Judy, you're getting ahead of yourself. If she'd been able to escape, she would've been home a very long time ago," Carl said. He ate a few bites before continuing. "It's like this—Nancy and Sharon went to Fergus Falls and located the suspect Jackson's grave. The two found a wall hanging picture with a man and a small boy on it in a diner. Someone in the diner relayed the news of where the man had lived. The two thought the picture looked like Jackson and they went to the abandoned farmhouse. They walked and poked around inside but didn't find anything."

"That's terrific, isn't it? But, who's the boy?"

"He is Bradley Gunderson, and he might be Vicky's son. He murdered his father but the lawyer got him off."

"There's something weird about that," Judy said. "How could he have a murder charge dropped? He would be forty-four now, right?"

"I presume Nancy and Sharon will tell the detectives?" Carl said.

"Yes. Most definitely, Nancy will tell them everything."

They finished eating.

"Any news about the area near the Soldier's Home?"

"From what I learned? No." Carl shook his head. "However, Nancy mentioned Will a few times and going to have coffee with him. Phone calls."

"Oh my. This sounds great. I wonder when she'll wear the Victoria's Secret purchase?"

"I don't even want to know." Carl grinned. "You three ladies are good for each other."

"Thank you for saying that. I agree. I'm also giving a great deal of thought to retiring and moving back to Minnesota. What do you think about that?"

"Frigid weather and all?"

"You betcha!"

"Let me think on that one, too."

Nancy
Chapter Twenty-two

The next few days slipped right by, an absolute whirlwind. Thanksgiving was just around the corner. I wondered what the Storbaekkene's and Sharon would be doing? I considered sending them an invitation when my phone rang. I reached for it and found it was Will.

"Nancy, I've got some great news to tell—guess what it is!"

"They've found her?" My eyes opened wide. "Tell me it's true."

"I'm starting to have a strong feeling that they've reopened the case. There may be enough new evidence for that to happen, and I owe it all to you," Will said. I felt his happiness through the phone. "However it turns out, at least we know we've done everything possible."

"It all started with Margo's death. Life has a way of multiplying wins and losses, doesn't it? Sometimes we hit a homer and then there's strike-outs. I hope the pictures, diaries, and your few items turned over to the investigators will lead them to her."

"My mother has perked up. It's like she's woken up from a deep sleep. For her sake, Vicky must be found."

"I've news for you that you can relay to Johnson."

"I'm all ears."

I went ahead and retold the story about Sharon and me going to Fergus Falls and what we discovered. I told him also about the picture in the diner.

"That's remarkable. I do have his number so I think I'll call him. He may just ring you back for more information."

"That's fine. I'll expect it."

We disconnected with me forgetting to mention Thanksgiving.

I went to the kitchen and made myself another pot of pressed coffee. I loved the aroma. Sitting by the kitchen table, with my phone nearby, I logged into my computer and started a search for Steve Turner. He still lived in the surrounding area. The investigation was underway, and I didn't want to mess anything up with Johnson, but I really wanted to contact Steve. It probably was best to wait until Johnson contacted me before I did any more, but it still niggled at me. Was he open to a relationship?

The next search on my mind was to go through the names of Roosevelt graduates from the school website. Sometimes names and address are given, family status, etc. I hoped to learn about Steve's children. A few minutes later, I discovered that in high school, he'd had several different girlfriends. As I compared his high school picture and a recent photo, it appeared as if he hadn't changed much except for the flock of silver hair. That was helpful should I see him somewhere. Also, he was now a respected architect and worked for a very well-known firm in the metro area. No further information was available. I delved further and found his address listed in the white pages. He lived nearby in one of the newer subdivisions. I made a mental note to seek his home out tomorrow after my haircut appointment and errands.

I jotted down what I knew about Steve. The next list I added the clues such as photos, diaries, and Will's items. Afterward, I wondered what next to research. Judy might have ideas. I decided to give her a call and hope that she answered. Instead, I left a voice mail.

The evening wore on until finally it was bedtime. I showered and as I climbed into bed, Sharon called.

"What's up?" I said.

"I'm going to come clean with the congregation on Sunday and Peggy will be there. Will you attend and sit by her? We'll need the support."

"Of course. What time?"

"Thanks so much. It's 10:00."

"Do I get a donut and coffee?"

"You stinker! Of course. Fellowship is always open."

"I'll be there."

Sunday was two days away. Sharon had to be a bundle of nerves. She'd feel better, I knew, but how brave and awful at the same time to have to declare your sexual preference. Why was it necessary? Why couldn't people be accepted for their deeds and love for one another?

I fell asleep with thoughts of Vicky hidden in a

cave or a locked room with only her bones left for discovery.

Morning came with a new outlook. I dreamed of locating Vicky and that Margo was somewhere nearby and directing my footsteps. It all sounded a little odd or goofy to me, but if it meant that my dear friend was leading me to our missing partner, then so much the better. I got up and dressed with vigor and went out to the kitchen sunshine. All was well. I knew Sharon already had confessed her sexuality to the bishop, but now she'd own her life. What a happy occasion.

As I drove to the hair stylist, I wondered if it was appropriate to purchase a gift for Sharon or should I look for a plant? Since it was getting near Christmas, I decided to purchase a poinsettia, a nice big red one. She'd always loved the season more than any other. There was a florist near Steve's house. That would be the last errand to run.

I finished with my breakfast and dressed for the weather before jumping into the car and backing from the driveway with the garage door closing behind me. The beauty shop was easily accessible, and I parked. Inside, I hung up my coat and sat. While I waited to be called, I weeded through my emails and then realized there was a voice mail from the police department. I was being asked to stop by the station for further questioning by Johnson. I responded with a text message, stating that I would meet him in an hour.

So much for well-laid plans.

After the haircut was finished, I went out the door to the car and started the engine. It didn't take long before I was on the highway and driving toward the police station. Once I'd arrived, an available parking space was a half-block away. In a short time, I was inside and let the reception know I was expected. Johnson greeted me and escorted me to his office.

"Have a seat."

"What's this about?" I asked, choosing the nearest chair.

"I want you to tell me in your own words what you remember of the conversation in the diner."

"It went like this—" I continued with the story and did my best to remember verbatim every word spoken, ending with the news that they didn't know who the mother was or where the boy was located.

"Well, the boy lives in Glenwood and works at one of the schools as a janitor. Thanks for the tip."

"Is that all you wanted to know?"

"Basically, yes, but I want to advise you to stop your snooping around and leave it to the authorities. You could be harming the investigation by going ahead. Once people open up, they don't like to repeat themselves or they change what they've said. The first time a witness speaks is usually more truthful, you see? Now when my guys spoke to the people in the diner, they got different answers. I realize it may have not been the same individuals, I'll grant you that, but stay out of our way, please."

"Have you looked into Steve Hunter again?"

"There you go again! Keep your nose out of police business before something awful happens to you."

"Did the fingernail and squirt gun from Will help

you?"

"Yes, the squirt gun helped with the elimination of prints. We're in the process of matching the squirt gun prints with known prints to identify Jackson's. The fingernail helped to positively identify Vicky's DNA. That's all I'm going to say."

"Okay. Am I dismissed?"

"Yes."

I stood to leave.

"Turn to the right, then follow the exit signs."

"Yes, sir."

I continued on my way to the car and was happy to sit inside of it. The heater warmed me up, and I waited a few more minutes to catch my thoughts and put all that I knew together. For some reason, Johnson was trying to scare me away from the investigation. It didn't seem right. Why? I glanced out of the side mirror to make sure the road was clear before driving away from the curb. My next destination was to locate Steve's house. In another few minutes, I entered the main road and drove toward the subdivision where I believed he lived.

The area at one time was a farm. Grain and cattle once grew on this land pheasants once inhabited as well as turkeys. Now the land held fortresses instead of a common, simple farm home. Children played indoors for hours on computers and the parents were too busy for boardgames and lasting relationships. The homes had large bedrooms, several bathrooms, play rooms, and a lovely backyard where, in the summers, they barbequed or lay in the sun. The size would've made me feel exceptionally lonely.

Traffic was light, and it didn't take long for me to locate the homes. I turned and slowly drove between two brick sidewalls. The homes were lovely and even though it was daylight, a few of the front trees had Christmas lights adorning them and were lit. Steve's house was easily found. I was correct in thinking it was huge. It didn't look as if he was home. I didn't see any childlike items in the yard such as a bicycle or swing set. His children may well be grown and gone by now, I knew, so it wasn't a great indication of family. I parked farther away, around the corner and shut off the car. As I pondered if I should walk past his house, a sporty type car entered the street and went toward the neighboring garage. I wondered if Steve had designed the homes, and if he'd owned the property? It was very likely he had. It caused me to pause. *If he built the house, where could Vicky be hidden?* I decided to park farther from the subdivision so as not to be seen. Since it was cold, I bundled up before climbing from the car.

The cold north wind took my breath away as I rounded the corner. Fortunately, the snow was only a few inches deep and easily manageable. During the walk toward the back and into a grove of trees nearby, I thought back to my youth and all the rides into the country with my family. Dad loved to go for Sunday afternoon drives. He especially liked this area because of the beautiful serenity of the animals and the workable land plus the colorful maple leaves in the fall. He'd point out various items along the way.

Suddenly I stopped. There was something about one certain day. What was it? Then I recalled that in this very grove we used to watch the cows drink from stock ponds. The fencing was broken and the cows were getting out and onto the road. Dad went up to the house to tell the occupants while Mom and I walked back to the car. *I remember watching the livestock drink.* The cold started to sink through my coat, cap, and gloves. I hurried back to my car.

I went about my business and picked up the few needed groceries and plant for Sharon before returning home. My thoughts were restless all night long.

I sent Judy a message inquiring about prom night and wondered how she was doing. She responded almost immediately.

Steve and Vicky seemed fine. Vicky danced once with Ron and that's all. I don't remember where Steve was at the time. He had been drinking. She rarely did but appeared to be "three sheets to the wind." That's all I know.

I responded: *I hadn't heard that about the dance nor the drinking. Could Steve had been drunk and abducted her? Then he didn't know what to do? Like take her to an out of the way place and leave her?*

Judy responded: *Anything is possible.*

We said, "Good night," and I puzzled over our conversation for the rest of the evening.

When morning came, I slipped into a dress and matching good shoes. After eating an egg and toast, it was time for me to go to Bethany and support Sharon. The traffic was wonderfully light and soon I parked on the side of the church and went inside. I found Peggy sitting in the front pew where I joined her. Sharon looked better than ever. Her eyes were bright, and she looked as if a huge load had been lifted from her shoulders. I smiled at her and gave her a thumbs up sign. She briefly nodded.

After the homily, Sharon informed the congregation about her retirement and that she was homosexual. She asked for prayers. Her last day would be in January so the board members had time to locate a new minister.

Silence filled the room. When the organist played the final hymn and Sharon exited, Peggy and I followed. Peggy and Sharon went to Peggy's, with me arriving behind them.

Peggy lived in south Minneapolis, not far from Sharon and in our same old neighborhood. Her house was on Nokomis Avenue, right near the Minnehaha creek bed. It was a beautiful two story home with all sorts of woodwork inside. The table was already beautifully set complete with chinaware and silverware. My poinsettia plant was a lovely centerpiece. The meal consisted of lasagna, salad, and garlic toast. It was delicious. The wine sparkled and was tasty.

"I'm glad that it's over," Sharon said. "It's a relief like no other."

"You did a wonderful sermon about acceptance and loving each other," I said.

"The reaction was phenomenal. No one spoke. Not during or afterward," Peggy said. "Did anyone say anything to you?"

"Not much, but no one wished me well. That says it all."

"Yes. It's time to move on," I said.

"I suppose you two already have plans for Thanksgiving?" I asked.

"I have my daughter and we'll be going to my mom's. Sharon, too."

"I think I'll volunteer once again at church for the meal. I've done it the last few years."

"You could join us," Sharon said.

"This is fine. Don't feel bad, I enjoy it."

After the cleanup Sharon and I sat in the living room for a few minutes while Peggy finished wiping the counters. I felt like she had something to tell me or else I would've helped longer in the kitchen.

"Nancy, I'm ready."

"I know it's about Mike, so go ahead." I snatched a tissue from my pocket. "Why did he marry someone else? Why not me? What happened?"

"He saw you and saw the prettiest, sweetest girl on earth. He loved you dearly, beyond words, but he knew he'd changed. The tour of 'Nam was awful. He'll forever be grateful for your help to transfer him from Vietnam during his second tour to the ship on the Mediterranean coast. You saved his life. Agent Orange covered him constantly. It entered his skin, he breathed it in. He knew he wasn't the same and couldn't give you what you wanted and deserved. He wanted to have a family before he left for his second tour but was so afraid of what would happen. Would his children be deformed? He couldn't bare it. Also, he didn't feel worthy of having children or being a good husband after all the killing. In the end, Agent Orange effected his brain, ate his insides and killed him. When his wife had her first pregnancy, the miscarriage was caused from Agent Orange. He has two children that he'll never see as adults. You were his first and true love. He wanted you to have a healthy family and to have a life you deserved, but you could never get him out of your heart. I think this is why you weren't satisfied in your marriage. Mike couldn't give all of himself to his wife, either. He never should've enlisted. He had mental health issues. PTSD really bad. He was a hoarder. He kept seeking help but little was forthcoming. That's why he was found frozen outside of the mental health facility for veterans.

"If only he'd given me a chance." Tears filled my eyes. "I dearly loved him. You're right, I shouldn't have married anyone else. He was the person I fell in love with, and I've hardly looked at anyone else."

"He wanted you happy." Sharon blew her nose.

"Thank you, Sharon."

We clung to each other.

"I haven't finished going through all of my mother's things. She'd always told me Mike had given her something for you but to wait until I felt the time was right. I never questioned her because it wasn't for me. There's two boxes left," Sharon said. She blew her nose. "You're forcing me into this. I've put off sorting Mom's belongings but now for you, I'm doing it."

"We're like sisters in many ways. Neither of us can

really talk about Mike, but I still love him."

"He died loving you," Sharon said. "When I discover what Mike left for you, I'll invite you over and you can open it in private." She smiled at me through her tears.

"I love you, Sharon."

We hugged as Peggy entered the room.

"Story told?" she asked. She carried in the last of the wine and three glasses.

"Yes. At last I know what happened to Mike."

"What a day," Sharon said. "Let's drink up."

The rest of the afternoon slipped away and then I headed for home.

Judy
Chapter Twenty-three

It was Thanksgiving and Carl and I were a couple once again. I was absolutely and positively pleased as punch. We'd even discussed remarriage. At last my life was coming together and I felt whole.

Since being discharged, I had resigned from teaching, I had not had a smoke, alcohol, or drugs of any kind. I felt like a brand new 409 engine ready to roll—only this time, the hubcaps were staying on good and tight. Instead of cleaning, I spent the extra spare hours in the kitchen. It had been a long time since this old girl baked a pie so I made four—two apple, a pecan, and a pumpkin. Yummy. I took in a deep breath because it smelled so darn good. Last, but not least, I put spice potpourri to simmer on the stove.

Walking to the living room, I noted it looked barely lived in. The pillows were plumped, the furniture vacuumed, and the walls gleamed from the wiping down. Over Christmas vacation, we planned to move all of Carl's things into my house.

I hurried to the bedroom and slipped into a new pair of jeans and my new Beatles t-shirt. I pulled my long brown, wavy hair to the side, clipping it back with a bow. My dangly blue earrings matched. As I gazed in the mirror one last time, I thought of myself as a young person and wondered where the years had disappeared.

While I checked on the turkey, Carl turned on Macy's Thanksgiving Day parade on the television. His mother was deceased, so it was just the two of us. I hadn't wanted to invite anyone else. I wanted Carl all to myself.

The turkey and dressing tasted delicious. Later in the evening, we turned the station to news just as Nancy called me.

She said, "Are you watching the news?"

The TV newscaster announced:

The investigation for a missing young woman, Vicky Storbaekkene, has been re-opened. She was abducted from her senior prom in 1970. This is her prom picture and what is believed that she'd look like today. Please call the number at the bottom of the screen if you know anything to help the case.

"Is that your Vicky?" Carl asked. I had turned the phone on speaker.

"Yes!" I cried. "Oh my gosh! The investigation! This is remarkable."

"Absolutely remarkable."

"Now what?"

"We'll have to wait and see." I waited for additional news until midnight.

Finally, we went to bed. I curled up beside Carl for comfort and warmth and felt safe but most of all—loved.

Nancy
Chapter Twenty-four

I woke to the smell of fresh coffee brewing and smiled. My heavier blue robe lay on the chair beside the bed, and I slipped into it. As I walked to the kitchen, something ticked in my mind, and I made an about-face. For some reason, it seemed like I needed to dress for the Antarctic. I slipped into a very warm woolen sweater, jeans with a pair of knee-length wool socks. Afterward, I went to the kitchen to pour juice and coffee. No sooner had I cracked an egg into the fry pan than my phone trilled. It was Will.

"Good morning," he said. "Are you up?"

"Good morning, and yes. Why?"

"They're doing something over at Steve Hunter's house. Something about a well."

"Oh my!"

"I'll pick you up in ten to fifteen minutes."

"Great!"

I hurried along the egg by turning up the temperature. In about two minutes flat, the egg was proportionately crisp around the edges but still acceptable to eat. I ate it in about two bites, chugged down the juice, poured my coffee into a to-go cup before putting on my coat. The timing was perfect. Will drove into the driveway just as I'd finished zipping up my boots.

As I stepped from the house, he honked. We were in sync.

"Perfect timing," I said. I climbed into the car and shut the door. As I buckled up, I said, "I went to Steve's before Thanksgiving and walked to the grove of trees out back where there once was the well and cattle used to graze."

"Farmland of old," Will said. "You've been busy snooping, I take it."

"Yep. I'm going to find your sister if it's the last thing I do. You and your mother—"

"And you, her friends."

"Thanks. We deserve to know what happened."

"Well, we'll have to tell him about your footprints, if he asks."

"I hope not. He's already gotten after me for putting my nose in where it doesn't belong."

"When we arrive, I'll tell him. We have to be upfront."

"I know. That's fine."

Will parked quite a distance from the area since by this time the closer spots were filled with media vans. All local stations had gotten wind of the new investigation. Reporters were armed with cameramen and microphones, ready to broadcast the event. We maneuvered around the media, somehow without being noticed, and stood near the crime scene tape after Will showed his identification to the uniformed officer protecting the site.

"Stay right here. I'll tell the detective you've

arrived," he said to Will. To me, he said, "You are?"

"Nancy Bjork."

While he went for Johnson, we watched the scene unfold. The well was uncapped and a man stood overhead pointing a search light into the hole.

"Ahh, Will and the sidekick, Nancy. I am glad you're here, but why do I have this feeling you're not surprised we're going to investigate this well?" Johnson looked right at me.

"Well, you see." I went into the rendition of Sunday drives with the family and seeing the animals grazing the field and in this very grove and drinking from the stock tanks.

"Ahh, huh. What else are you not telling me?"

"That I walked the area the day before Thanksgiving. If you see prints in the snow, they're mine."

"Did you find anything, Miss Nosy?"

"Nope. It was too cold to snoop. I went home."

"Is that all?"

"Yes."

Will chuckled, and I nudged him.

"Keep an eye on her, Will. If she moves, I want to know."

"Got it."

Johnson shook his head at me before he returned to the well.

As we stood watching, the crowd behind started speaking louder but neither of us turned around. I didn't want anyone to zero in on me, and Will had had enough reporters invading his privacy over the years.

We took turns squeezing each other's hands for warmth. Occasionally placing our arms across each other's shoulders. It seemed forever until finally an officer returned to tell us that bones were found and were being brought to the surface. He didn't want to speculate if they were human or not.

"Will you be here much longer? We're starting to freeze up," I asked a nearby officer.

"No. I can assure you this will be closed up again relatively soon," the officer responded.

"Okay. Detective Johnson, I assume, will contact me once he's sure of what they are?"

"Yes. The detective will expedite the case."

"Thanks."

We held hands as we trudged back through the crowds, avoiding the media. WCCO, the local station, caught up to Will, but he shrugged them off. We kept moving until able to climb into the car. I shivered all the way home.

"Come in for hot chocolate. It'll warm you up."

"Not a bad idea."

He put the car in park and shut the engine off, following me indoors.

"Brr!" I said, going into the kitchen. "Let me take your coat."

"I can do it."

We took care of ourselves and then I went about heating up a piece of chocolate inside a mug filled with milk. When they were steamy hot, I placed a spoon in each and carried them to the living room where I found him, half asleep.

"The cold makes you sleepy or is it that the warmth after freezing does?"

"Either one." Will stirred his cup and took a sip from it. "You know, I feel different. Around you, I feel so relaxed. And now, hopefully, finding my sister, I almost feel as if I can live again. Without her, all these years, I've felt lost and lonesome. Like a part of me is gone."

"I feel good around you, Will. I'm not saying that lightly, either. I really hope our renewed investigation of finding Vicky will have an ending. Good or bad. Not that I want her dead and bones found, I'd rather have her alive."

"I know what you're saying. Either way, at least there will be a closure. Mom hasn't been herself the last few years. She's in her eighties. I'm willing to bet she's been holding onto life because of wanting Vicky found. It's like she's waiting to die for the right moment."

"Like a husband dying and the wife within days. It's all love."

"Exactly." Will sipped from his mug as did I. We watched the snow begin to fall. "Tell me about Sharon's brother. Mike, is it? What happened?"

"I fell for Mike like a ton of bricks. I could never shoo him from my mind. I couldn't give my husband the love he needed, wanted and deserved because my heart was always with Mike. I do feel bad about that, and I'm glad that Paul has found someone that truly loves him for who he is. It's not much different from your marriage falling apart. We both were in a sort of limbo and afraid to love or give of ourselves to another person for fear of losing them."

"We are pretty similar, aren't we?"

"Yes. Sharon finally admitted to me Mike wasn't the same man when he returned, that he wasn't the same person. He also had a second tour of Vietnam that I assisted his mom with the help of Humphrey's office to get him reassigned to a ship to complete his assignment." I finished my hot chocolate. "You see, Sharon admitted to me that Mike had said I was the love of his life. I was the prettiest, sweetest, and kindest girl he'd ever met and still innocent. Because of the Agent Orange after effects, he didn't feel right marrying me. Agent Orange took his life by eating his insides and his brain. PTSD took over his mind. He's been dead almost ten years." I sighed. "At least now, I know the truth. She has something for me in with her mother's things, and she'll let me know when she finally unearths them it. I'm happy now. I feel a relief. I've always wondered if it was something I did or was it just me, and that's why he broke the engagement. Wasn't I pretty enough? Or wasn't he attracted to me anymore? See, I put it all on myself."

"The truth will set you free."

"And, it has. Now I'm open to my life. To experience all that there is."

"Me too," Will said. He leaned toward me and we kissed. When he broke away, he said, "That was nice."

"I thought so too." Tears filled my eyes. I hadn't been kissed so tenderly for so many years I'd forgotten what it felt like.

"I should go and see my mother before going back to the office. She's waiting to hear what all happened."

"Why don't you call her while I make a grilled cheese sandwich for us both. I'm hungry and you must be too."

While Will spoke to his mom, I made our meal. When we'd finished, Will thanked me and left for work. He did give me another sweet kiss, which made me feel warm all over. I went about my business of cleaning house but kept the local news station on the TV in case there'd be more breaking reports. When I'd finished, I sent a text message to Judy and Sharon to tell them about the morning's episode at the well.

Judy responded: *That does it! I'm leaving Madison and coming there.*

I responded: *What about Carl?*

Judy's response: *I'll call later. Keep me informed.*

I said: *I will.*

I did question about mentioning Will's kiss but decided to keep it to myself to savor.

Sharon rang me up on the phone.

"I saw it on the news."

"I went with Will. He picked me up this morning."

"How's he doing?"

"Good. We talked for quite a while. He's had it tough. We're pretty equal with our emotions about events in our lives."

"Judy's probably going to come," Sharon said.

"Yes. It sounds like it. Should I offer her to stay here?"

"She's off drugs and alcohol. It won't be a problem

anymore and Carl will be with her."

"That's true. It won't be a repeat of the last time."

"I have Peggy here and she's motioning me over."

"If there's anything else, I'll let you know."

We disconnected and I sent a message to Judy. I told her the code to my garage and that the room was available for her and Carl to stay in.

I got myself ready for the evening shows and watched an old Christmas movie: *It's a Wonderful Life* before going to bed.

At six, my phone interrupted my sleep. It was Will once again.

"Are you up?" he said.

"I am now. Why?"

"Be at my house in an hour. No need to dress like an Eskimo."

"Okay."

Of course, I didn't know what this escapade was about, but I wasn't going to miss out on it. I dressed hurriedly, slipping on pants and a sweater. Once my hair was combed and teeth brushed, I grabbed my purse and put on my coat and shoes. Once in the car, I drove to the nearest drive-thru and got a coffee and a roll so the sugar and caffeine would kick-start my brain. In just under an hour, I parked outside of his house. Will had his car out and started. When he saw me climbing from my car, he came out of his front door.

"What's this all about?"

"The beginning of the end."

Judy
Chapter Twenty-five

The message last night from Nancy was hopeful for discovering Vicky. Carl reminded me I still didn't have my driver's license and attended Alcohol Anonymous meetings that were court ordered. The very first thing that entered my head was seventy days sober. With each day drug and alcohol free, my spirit became lighter. I was happier than I'd been in years.

Right away in the morning, I made an appointment with my attorney. Carl drove but wouldn't attend the meeting. He wanted me to take full responsibility for everything and not lean on him. He'd still support me from the waiting room. Why had I let my life get so out of control? Why hadn't I turned my back on my parents, family, everyone that made my life miserable?

I now had my friends back and most importantly, I had Carl's love and trust. Now I had friends and a lover who knew all about me but didn't judge. My spirit was refreshed.

During the meeting, it was decided I could leave the area for a short time but was expected to return for the AA meeting in three days. I explained how badly I wanted to be with my friends in case of Vicky's discovery.

"What happened?" Carl asked when I entered the waiting room.

"We can go to Minneapolis but I must return to attend the next AA meeting."

"Sounds good."

Carl walked me out to the car. As he held it open for me to climb inside, he said, "I still love those legs of yours."

"*Oh*!" I smiled. "That sounds sexy."

"Let's pack and go. We can spend the night near Minneapolis. It'll give us time together before all the commotion—if they have found her."

"I want to be with my friends when this happens."

Just then my phone dinged a message from Nancy.

I'm with Will and we're driving north.

"Let's hustle. The investigation is popping."

Nancy
Chapter Twenty-six

With my coffee cup in hand, I settled in for the long drive north. Fortunately, the weather had warmed and it was a mere twenty-five degrees.

"I'm at a loss for words for how far this investigation has gone," I said. "Where are we going and why isn't your mom with us?"

"I haven't said much to her. I don't want her hopes up, but I have a feeling—a good one—about this lead. That boy you saw in the picture, you and Sharon?"

"Yes. Don't tell me he's been found?"

"More than that," Will said. He entered the Interstate 94W entrance. "We're going to Glenwood where he'll be formally interviewed."

"Oh my word! How did this all come about so quickly?"

"First off, the found bones yesterday at the well were from animals, probably cattle. No human remains were among them."

"Okay. That's good to know." I drank more of my coffee.

"That boy saw it on the news and called the local police station about his mother."

"I presume his name was on record because of the murder of his father?"

"Yes, and that became a 'red' alert, so to speak," Will said. He smoothly went around cars and steered back into the proper lane. "Something about not knowing who his mother really was or who he was and no family. He thought his mother might be the missing Vicky Storbaekkene."

"Do you know if she's alive or where she'd be?"

"No. No clue." Will shook his head and gripped the steering wheel. "I'm a bundle of nerves."

"I can see why and also your reasoning for not keeping your mother in loop. She must be suspicious, though?"

"I think she is because I haven't called her like usual or come around," Will said. "I could use a different topic to keep me focused on driving."

"What should we talk about?"

"I'd like to hear more about Mike. It's fascinating to know that you sort of lived your life like I did. If we start having a relationship, I want everything in the open. I'll talk more about me later, let's begin with you."

"Mike had flashbacks, I believe they were beyond comprehension. Sharon hinted a long time ago he had little to do with the family. The kiss they got from him before he left for his second tour wasn't tender. He'd also acted mean, like telling his sister's how ugly they were or their clothes weren't right. He seemed to hate everything his mom fixed for him even his favorite Irish stew. I don't think he was ever the same."

"There's plenty of people whose life changed because of the war. Marriages. Children. Hatred and violence. Drugs and alcohol abuse due to the fighting and not wanting to remember what had happened. It's a dirty shame."

"I lost my first love to the war. I'm a casualty because of how it affected his mind and body that prevented us from a marriage. I hoped with all of my heart we'd be back together." I finished my coffee and set the empty cup into the space provided. "Your turn."

"I lost my wife and it was my fault completely. I couldn't love her the way she needed. Jealousy prevailed and realization of abandonment overtook my good senses and I began to stalk her. First, I hired an investigator because she worked late hours at the bank. How can a banker have such late hours? It made no sense. Meetings too, going to other cities with bank reps. To me, it added up to an affair. I was positive."

"Did she?"

"No. It was on the up and up. It was me and my fear of being alone. My paranoia. I probably will always have some of that inside of me, even if we are able to locate Vicky. Do you realize how many years? Forty-eight." He stared out of the windshield.

"Take some deep breaths," I said and did the same. "We're coming to an end."

"Yes. And it's all due to you and your friends."

"No. It's a collaboration of us all, including you and your mother. Without you and your few items plus your mom wanting this to happen, we wouldn't be here." I smiled. "But it's not over."

"It will be soon. I can feel it."

"Agreed."

I was sure Mike was smiling down on me.

"We understand each other, thoroughly."

"Yes," I said.

In just short of an hour, Will exited from the interstate and we got onto Highway 55, which brought us to the small hamlet of Glenwood. Lake Minnewaska was the heart of the town. On the opposite end was the town of Benson where honest farmers worked from sunrise to sunset. He followed the signs to the police station that was near the church, library, and grocery store plus the funeral home. He parked and we went inside.

Someone ushered us to the interrogation observation room where we were met by Johnson.

"You too? I might've known," he said to me. "It's just as well."

"If either of you have a question that may be pertinent to the investigation, tell Officer McCloskey." He nodded toward the officer. "He'll talk into his mic and I'll hear it. If I find it relevant, then it'll be repeated."

"I can think of one question, right now," I said.

"What's that?"

"If she wore a hairclip, where would it be placed?"

"What was her favorite color?" Will said.

"Okay, good ones. The answers?"

"Above her right ear."

"Purple."

"My given name, Olaf. See if he knows that."

"Okay. Let's get started."

Will reached out his hand and took mine, squeezing it, and I squeezed back as we stared into the one-way glass. I glanced at Officer McCloskey who stood beside me with a mic clipped onto his collar. My heart pounded and I was pretty sure Will's was also. We watched as the middle-aged man was ushered into the small interrogation room. He sat so we could see him, with Johnson's back to us. An officer stood guard beside the man.

His name was Bradley, which was a name Vicky had liked and was Steve's middle name. Bradley's forehead reminded me of Diane's and Vicky's. Will's wasn't quite as wide. His eyes were small and inset, similar to Will's. His hands were large and so were Will's. The height of both men was similar.

The questioning began with his full name. The last name was Gunderson. His dad was Jackson Gunderson. I didn't need to hear anymore. I began to weep and Will pulled me closer, keeping his arm across my back. His breathing was shallow as if he held it back, afraid of what was to come.

Finally Johnson asked our two questions, and Bradley answered as clear as a bell:

"Behind her right ear. Purple."

"How come you never tried to get in touch? You must've had some knowledge of a family or where your mother was from."

"Mom said she was from Minneapolis. She wasn't allowed to say much, not around Jackson. She did tell me her name, Storbaekkene and her brother's name, Will. I did look in the phone books for Minneapolis and St. Paul for them but couldn't locate any in the metropolitan area."

"How do you spell Storbaekkene?"

"S-t-o-r-e-b-a-k-e-n. Storebaken."

"That's your first mistake, you didn't have it spelled correctly."

"I never knew." Tears clouded Bradley's eyes and he wiped them. "How could I have known. If Mom wrote something down, I never would've seen it. There's little or no trace left of her. Social services stepped in once she was hospitalized, and I was sentenced to the juvenile training center."

"Tell me about your life," Johnsons asked.

"Mom was never allowed out of the house. When he'd go somewhere, we'd be locked in the basement in an enclosed room without running water or proper food."

"What happened when he returned?"

"He'd beat us. Mom was almost always bruised and he'd broken her arm. I can still remember her scream. I tried to set it. She told me what to do."

"What about school?"

"I walked. No friends. My clothes were always dirty and smelly. My hair greasy because of no running water. Thin as a rail."

"What happened the last time that you saw your father? Jackson?"

"I hit him over the head with the shovel he'd used on Mom and me. Mom was unconscious when I came home from school. That's how I found her. On the floor, barely breathing. He was drunk and passed out on the couch. I was so angry I took the shovel and hit him over the head, then called the police."

"Where is your mother now?"

"In a nursing home. I've waited for this day for many years. I couldn't let her go until I found my true family. I received treatment for anger and other social problems like trust and how to interact properly with adults. I had regular meetings with psychologists and had good teachers. Now I live nearby and work as a janitor in a school."

Will and I glanced at each other and held each other tighter.

"She prophesied this happening," I whispered.

Will nodded.

Will leaned into the officer and whispered something to him.

"Do you know Olaf?"

"I remember her whispering that name a few times but I don't know why."

"It's your uncle's given name. Olaf William, and he's called Will."

"No wonder why I couldn't find Mom's family. I didn't have the last name or the first correct."

"What was your mom's favorite toy as a child, do you know?"

"Barbie doll."

"I have a nephew. I have family." Will smiled. "Now I wish Mom was here."

Bradley was ushered from the room by the officer standing guard. Johnson came around to speak to us.

"It sounds good," Will said. "I can see my sister in

him."

"Don't get your hopes up yet. Just because he answered correctly doesn't mean he's related to your family. We need positive identification, which brings me to you." Johnson waited a beat. "We need to match your DNA results with his."

"We're finished for now?" Will said.

"Yes. Now it's up to science and not little Miss Nosy." He grinned.

"Thanks." I grinned.

"I'm hungry but don't feel like I can eat much," Will said. "How about you?"

"I feel the same. There's an A&W right up on the hill we'd passed coming into town."

"Let's go."

The meal of a hamburger basket and fries went to waste. Neither of us had much to say. I thought about Bradley and how awful his life had been. I wanted to hug him tight and never let him go. Will looked at me through moist eyes while we picked at our food.

"Let's go. This was a rotten idea," Will said. "I want to take Bradley home with me."

"I want to hug him until all the hurt goes away."

We picked up our sodas and left the restaurant.

"I wonder where Vicky is?" I asked. Will had started driving toward home. "I want to see her again, but I'm afraid."

"It sounds like she's alive, doesn't it?" Will said. "I bet she's somewhere in Glenwood."

"Probably, but they won't tell us until they're positive."

"Right, but I think they've put this case on the fast lane."

"Me too."

I got home early evening and was happy to be home. I sent a message to both Sharon and Judy to keep them informed. Both responded stating they wanted to be with me when we were able to locate her. Judy planned to arrive later in the evening.

After showering, I made myself a cup of hot chocolate before sitting down for a short while. I wasn't ready to sleep so I turned the television on, surfing the stations until settling upon a Ken Burns Public Broadcast Special on National Parks. It looked interesting.

Sharon sent a message, and I told her to come over right away.

The doorbell rang, and I got up to answer it.

"Come in, you two." Judy and Carl stood on my doorstep. I stepped aside for them to enter, shutting the door afterward. "I'm so happy you're here." I kissed them both. "Your room's down the hallway. Make yourself at home"

When they'd refreshed themselves and returned to the living room, I told them about the days' events.

"I'm glad we're here," Judy said. "We're going to find her alive."

"I hope so, but in what state?" Carl said. "What about this Bradley?"

"He seems like a decent young man. He must be in his mid-forties."

"Well, we must assume she was raped a number

of times. I really feel for her and wish we would've put our heads together sooner. Maybe we could've found her in time, before whatever has happened to her happened. You know? Poor thing."

"Yes. I've thought that, also." The phone rang, and I answered to Will. "Judy and Carl are here. Sharon's on the way."

"Thanks. I wondered. I'd come but I need to stay with Mom."

We disconnected.

Judy popped popcorn, and we sat around watching an old movie on Netflix. Half-an hour later, Sharon arrived. She opted for the couch, but I told her to sleep in with me. After midnight, we were ready to pack in and go to sleep.

Of course, I didn't sleep and I know Sharon didn't either. I suspected that no one did, including Will.

When the phone rang at 5:00, I knew it was Will.

"We're all here and having a slumber party. What's up?"

"I'm picking up Mom in an hour and going to the Glenwood nursing home. We'll be there about eleven. Give us a little time alone with her."

"I take it the DNA matched?"

"Yes. They wanted to seal up and close the investigation asap. Bradley will also be there."

"Okay. Good. You and your mom have our prayers. Drive safely and we'll meet you there."

"You too."

I nudged Sharon who immediately sat up.

"I'm getting dressed."

"I am waking Judy and Carl."

I knocked on the door and within seconds heard, "We're up. The phone woke us and can only mean one thing."

"Exactly. We leave in less than an hour."

"We're boogie-ing."

"Carl? Your car's in front of the door. You'll have to move it."

"I'll drive."

It wasn't long before we'd jumped into the car. Carl drove through and paid for coffee and rolls for us all. Judy gave him the directions. In a short time, we parked in front of the nursing home and went inside.

We needn't have asked which room she was in because of the spectacle of police and reporters in front of the door.

The three of us held hands as we walked the hallway toward the room with Carl holding up the rear. We locked our arms together as we fought our way to the forefront of the crowd. Diane lay beside Vicky in bed, cuddling close. Bradley and Will were nearby. Will saw us peering inside and motioned for us to enter.

"Your mom's friends. Nancy, Judy, and Sharon."

We hugged him tightly.

In unison, we said, "We loved your mom and have missed her dearly."

We took turns hugging him again with tear-stained eyes.

"Mom, let the girls see her."

The room nurse helped Diane scooch back. Vicky

had never regained consciousness and was in a fetal position. The pretty Vicky we knew was deep inside of her. Her body had wasted to the size of a child from lack of living. We were positive all the love she'd stored up while lying unconscious for so many years was waiting to come out. We each enveloped our friend within the folds of our arms and passed all of our love into her.

We stayed for just a few minutes before leaving so the family could reacquaint with each other.

"We have our friend."

"We have the end," Sharon said.

"Not yet," Judy said. "I haven't worn my Victoria's Secret purchase. Has anyone else?"

"No."

"No."

"Then, the best is yet to come."

Carl looked at Judy, who winked.

Judy
Chapter Twenty-seven

After returning to Nancy's house, Sharon stayed for a short while before she left for home. We were elated to have finally found Vicky but glum at the same time. I'm not sure what we had expected, but seeing her now seemed to have taken the juice out of us. We all were tired and took to our beds early.

When the morning came, we said our goodbyes, and Carl and I left.

We were certain that the family would contact us if there was any change in her condition, and I needed to be home for the AA meeting.

"This is wonderful, Carl. You and me alone. By ourselves. Driving down the road going home. I couldn't be happier."

"You know what? You've changed. You're the same girl I fell in love with so many years ago." He reached for my hand.

"You have faith in me."

"You bet I do. I'll help you through it all." He steered the car onto the main thoroughfare. "What are your thoughts about Vicky and the kid?"

"I think life sure has a lot of bends and twists, but I do believe Bradley and Will will be happy together as family, and I predict something to come between

Will and Nancy. I'll be very happy for them both if that happens."

"You might be on to something between those two, or should I say three?"

"I wonder when they'll disconnect the life-support?"

"Give them time. I'm sure that you'll have another chance to say your goodbye."

"Possibly. Diane and Will will want to spend time with her before that happens, I think."

"She looked frail."

"Diane looked better at the funeral than now. Time has taken its toll on her health."

"How old is she?"

"In her eighties."

I closed my eyes and slept for the rest of the way home. Once we arrived, we spent little time putting away our things and getting a bite to eat. Carl kissed me but not before pulling me into his arms. "I'm never letting you go."

The kiss knocked my socks off.

"Wow!" I looked into his eyes and saw goodness.

We climbed into bed after spending the next hour having sex. It felt good, like when we first married, to make love before kissing good night.

Nancy
Chapter Twenty-eight

It had been a week since Vicky was discovered and I hadn't heard from Will. I'd left him a few voice mails and sent messages, but he never responded. I had a feeling he'd contact me soon, but no way of knowing. The days lingered on and I tired of sitting and waiting for the phone to ring or watching old movies. I'd read two books and was about to open my third mystery when Sharon called to invite me over. She'd finally finished weeding through her mother's belongings and found what she was looking for—the last of Mike's correspondence.

I put on my coat and cap, grabbed my purse, and headed out the door for Sharon's house.

She opened the door as I walked up to it and we gave each other a huge hug.

"Have a seat and get comfy," She said. "I'll pour us a cup of coffee. Cookies are on the coffee table."

"Sounds good." I curled up on the couch, pulling a throw over myself. My heart pounded with anticipation. I couldn't wait to see his handwriting once again. I still wished we'd married but was feeling better and accepting his loss much easier than I had before Margo's funeral. When Sharon returned, I took the hot mug with my shaking fingers. "I'm excited and nervous all at the same time."

"I don't blame you."

"Where should we begin?" I asked. "From the top?"

"This is what I remember: Mike said that when he saw you standing there at Snyder's Drug Store, he fell in love all over again."

"Why didn't he tell me this? Why didn't he give me a chance? We loved each other." I blew my nose.

"What were his words to you? Can you remember?"

"'I'm not the same person.' That's what he said. I didn't understand at the time." I wiped my eyes.

"You were only seventeen."

"We were passionate for each other."

Tears streamed down our cheeks.

"That last time I saw him, he lived alone. It was the Fourth of July when I went to see him. You'll never guess how I found him." Sharon placed her arm over my shoulders and pulled me closer. "He had a rifle and was under the kitchen table, hollering at the Asian people outside of his window. He lived in a trailer court near his kids. I had to calm him down. After a while, he went to his chair, then we talked."

"Oh, my God."

"Major flashbacks. He was one of those hoarders. We had to rent a dumpster. He was my hero."

"Mine, too."

Tears filled our eyes as we spoke.

"It had to have been a horrible life for him," I said. "I can't imagine not being in control of your own life."

"If he'd lost you because of a divorce or experienced too many flashbacks, he'd never have been able to stand it. He didn't want you to see him suffer. He was very much in love with you."

"I feel so awful for him. He was such a good man. Good person, kind and gentle."

"That's how you must remember him." Sharon handed me a pile of letters. "Mom put this aside for you."

"You're kidding?"

"Nope. It's something Mike gave her to keep until the right time."

I smiled and took them. "His handwriting. I can't believe it."

It read:

Dear Mom,

I know I haven't been around much, but I still love you and Dad just like I always have. Please do this favor for me. Since I'm not healthy, I'd like for you to keep this letter for Nancy. There's a gift for her, too. Please don't let her see this letter or the gift until either I'm gone or you are. In that case, maybe Sharon can give this to her.

Your loving son,

Michael.

"After all these years. I really don't know what to say." I sucked in a breath. "I'm ready for it." I took the envelope addressed to me.

It read:

My dearest Nancy,

I'm very, very much in love with you to this day. I couldn't bring myself to marry such a pretty, sweet, innocent, young woman. I wanted to build my life with you but knew it wouldn't work because of my experiences in Vietnam. I can't thank you enough for loving me.

My love holds no bounds for you. My heart has hugged you forever.

I do hope that you've been able to have a good life.

I do have something for you, which I'm unable to give you myself. If you want it, fine. If not, it's yours to do with as you please. I had bought this for you and couldn't bring myself to give it to another woman.

You're mine for always.

Love forever. Love holds no boundaries.

Your soldier boy,

Mike.

"I didn't know. Oh my God." Tears spilled from my eyes onto the letter. I handed it over to Sharon to read. After, we held each other tight.

It seemed a very long time before she said, "Better?"

"I don't know. This sure answers everything, doesn't it?" I reached for the small box. "This is really more than I ever expected."

"Open it," Sharon said.

I waited a moment, then tore the paper from the outside. Inside the box was a ring.

"I don't believe it," I whispered as I removed the diamond engagement ring. "It's beautiful. We would've been married for forty-five years now."

"You two always have been married."

"But I didn't know it," I said.

"We'd tucked each other inside of our hearts and

never let the other go," I said. "Truly, we are sisters."

"Yes, we are," Sharon said.

I slipped the ring onto my finger.

"What should I do with it? I certainly can't wear it on my ring finger. I'd like to wear it as a remembrance."

"Put it on your right hand."

"I knew I was right all these years. People told me different. I quit talking about him because it wasn't worth it or it hurt too much."

"Right about what?"

"That his heart was true. He did love me—and even though he's up there," I looked up toward the heavens, "he still loves me. He's waiting for me."

"You bet he is." Sharon watched me unclasp my necklace and slip the end through the ring, placing it around my neck. "Good place for it."

"Now, I have Mike's never ending love over my heart."

The tragedy of our lives finally made sense.

I spent the rest of the day with Sharon looking at old pictures and talking about old times and our lives. When finally I drove home, I was at peace.

And when I tucked myself into bed, I fell fast asleep.

At 8 o'clock AM Will gave me a call.

"I have bad news. I'm sorry for starting this way, but I don't know the right way of telling you this."

"I'm sitting down. I'm ready."

"Mom passed away two days ago. Yesterday Vicky's life-support system was removed. Funeral arrangements need planning, and we're considering putting the two in a larger coffin, if possible, simply because—"

"That's lovely. Do you want me to be with you?"

"Please?"

"Tell me where and when you want me."

He told me what time at the mortuary. I was to meet him at ten at his house, and he also wanted me to join him later at his mother's. Bradley planned to be with us. Will was nervous and wanted to make sure the arrangements were perfect for the two most beautiful and loving women he'd ever known.

"I'll owe you for this," he said.

"You owe me nothing. It's the least I can do for you and your family. I'll see you soon."

"Thank you."

After disconnecting, I sent a group message to Sharon, Judy, and Carl to let them know what I'd just learned.

I dressed in a pair of black dress pants and a red sweater set with a decorated scarf for adornment. My earrings matched the scarf—snowflakes. After using the facilities, I fried an egg and had my morning brew.

As I slipped into my winter coat, both responded.

Judy said: *I'm going to get special permission to leave for the funeral since I'm still on parole for drinking and driving and must attend meetings. Let me know the information asap.*

Sharon said: *I'm officiating. The date's not set yet. Presumably on Friday.*

I said: *I'll know everything at the end of the day and so*

will Sharon. Got to run. XO

I finished buttoning up and went out to the car.

As drove from the neighborhood, I passed by newly formed snowmen and lights on outside trees and along porch rails. Christmas was definitely in the air. Fortunately, it wasn't snowing and blowing so the drive was peaceful into south Minneapolis. I had a few minutes so I drove near my old high school and by the Riverview Theater before going to Will's house.

Will opened the door as soon as he saw me and hugged me close to his chest.

"Thanks," he whispered in my ear.

"Anything for you." He kissed me lightly on the cheek.

Turning to Bradley, he said, "Do you remember Nancy?"

"Yes. Mother mentioned names once in a while, and yours was one of them," Bradley said. He smiled shyly. "I'm having a hard time putting everything together after all of these years."

"I bet you are," I said. "Now you have family. An uncle and you did meet your Grandma. That's a blessing."

"Yes. And I did manage to take a picture of Brad with Mom and one with Vicky. He took one of me with Vicky. Pictures all around."

"That's great. Memories that are worth holding in your heart."

"We need to get going," Will said. He looked at his watch. "We're almost late."

Will drove and in fifteen minutes we were seated

in the office. I listened as they discussed expenses and the possibility of the two women lying side-by-side in a coffin since both were petite in stature. The flower arrangements were chosen for the funeral before we went down to choose which casket would fit the need. After one was decided upon, Sharon was contacted and the funeral arrangements were set in stone.

As soon as we left, my phone dinged. Sharon sent a group message that informed us of the time and date. I was glad she had because now Judy had more time to plan her escape from Madison and the clutches of AA meetings. I knew she needed to go to them, but this funeral was important. I had a feeling the world was going to open for me, Judy, and Sharon. That time had stood still once for me but was now ready to speed ahead full blast.

"We're almost at Mom's. Bradley? You're welcome to keep anything of your mom's or grandma's as a remembrance. We'll mark it."

"Thanks, this is more than I could ever hope for."

"Where do you work? What are your plans?" I asked.

"I couldn't be far from Mom. I took online courses but could never follow through to earn the needed credits toward teaching. I want to be a math teacher. The teachers at the juvenile training center helped me tremendously. They said I was a math 'whiz kid.'"

"That's spectacular," I said. "Your mom was good in math. I used to cheat and look at her answers. How do you think I passed algebra?"

Will chuckled.

"Are you still seeing a counselor for all that's happened to you?" I asked. "You should, if you're not."

"I do go to a group session once a month at the mental health facility. It relieves the pressure of Mom and what's happened to me. Now that I have a family, I'm already feeling a hundred times better."

"That's wonderful," I said.

"I'll keep going for some time."

"I'd like for you to move closer, Bradley. You could live with me, and there are plenty of mental health facilities in Minneapolis. I'm sure your counselor could recommend several. There are jobs all around that you can apply for and take classes. You can do this until you get your feet on the ground."

"That sounds marvelous," I said.

At Diane's house, Will parked in the garage since she hadn't owned a car for a few years.

Once inside, we walked through the rooms together. Will pointed to paintings and photographs and told us about them. In Diane's room, on the dresser was a photo of Vicky in her prom dress as well as her senior picture and from grade school. Pictures of her with friends and family.

"Mom wanted to see her family before she closed her eyes for the last time," Will said.

"You mean, she wanted them in her heart and mind in case she died," I said. "When did your mom put all these pictures here on her dresser? Usually pictures like this are scattered around the house or on the living room wall or down the hallway."

"Ever since Margo's funeral, she started. She'd say things like, 'I know she's alive.' 'When she dies, I will too.' Weird things like that."

"She had premonitions."

"The pictures of my mother are amazing. I'd like copies of them and Grandma."

"You will. I'll see to it," Will said.

"Yes," I said.

Will opened the closet where her clothes hung.

"I always liked her in this dress." He held up a blue flowered dress. "I know it's winter and this is a summer dress."

"If your mom wore this dress often," I nodded toward it, "then she should be buried in it. You'll have a peaceful memory."

"I appreciate you and your sound advice," Will said. He placed the dress over his arm and led us to Vicky's room.

"It's identical after all these years to what it had been when we were kids. The flowered bedspread and the wall hangings of the Beatles. Wow!" I opened her closet, which revealed her dresses. I removed a beautiful pink dress and said, "This was her favorite. She'd sewn it in home economics class. I sewed one also, only it was blue. She'd like to be buried in it." I handed it over to Will who took it but gave it to Bradley.

After the walk through, we stood near the front door.

"I won't get started clearing this all out right away, but we need to get it on the market. The sooner the better." Will looked at Bradley and said, "You'll get your mother's half."

"I can't expect that. It's not right."

"It is, though," Will said. "You kept my dear sister and mother alive for many years. You gave my mother hope for a grandchild, hope for the future, hope to see her daughter again. We were able to circle our arms around Vicky and give her the love she'd missed for years, so she could take it with her to her death. Love is the key. You loved your mother so much, you gave her the lasting legacy of love and being cherished. You allowed her to receive it from her family and friends. You are my hero."

Tears flooded our eyes.

After we'd dried our eyes, Will drove us back to his house. I left immediately for home and time alone to remember good times of dances, boyfriends, slumber parties but most of all enjoying a much simpler life of love and laughter.

Judy
Chapter Twenty-nine

As I was almost finished cooking supper, Carl still hadn't come back home. The meatloaf was browned, the baked potatoes done, and the bag of corn, microwaved. I'd worked hard on this meal, and it was ready to start drying up like a prune. Where was he?

I set the table, including napkins and placemats.

I checked messages once again and found the date and time for the funeral. Carl wasn't included in the group, which didn't surprise me. He wasn't one of us silly little girls from way back when. He was here and now.

Since we'd be leaving right away in the morning for Minneapolis, I left the food to fend for itself and went to the bedroom to pack. Was it the right time to pack my Victoria's Secret purchase? I stuffed it down under my other underwear and placed a sweater over it before adding more clothes. When finished, I heard the back door open and close.

"Judy, I'm home!"

"Be right there!"

I closed the suitcase and went to the kitchen. On the table was a spray of roses.

"They're lovely." I leaned over to smell them. "Carl? What would I do without you?"

"I'm not sure, but will you marry me again?"

"In a heartbeat."

We kissed deeply and then Carl placed a diamond on my ring finger.

"It's beautiful. It's more than I ever hoped for. I've always loved you."

"It goes without saying."

We kissed again. Afterward, I dished up our meal.

"Fascinating. Meatloaf," Carl said. He grinned. "Some thing's never change."

"We should take cooking classes someday."

"It's a deal."

We kept eating, but I could tell he itched to tell me more news by the way he shoveled down the food.

"What else is on your mind?" I asked.

"I've contacted Sharon, and I hope you don't mind—"

"Spill it!"

"The day after the funeral, she accepted my request to officiate our wedding. She also has news for us but plans to tell us later."

"You're kidding! Sharon? That's wonderful!" My eyes opened wider. "Marry! So soon! Yes!"

"I thought you might like my idea."

"So, it's the funeral and then the following day at Bethany? What time will the ceremony be performed?"

"Ten in the chapel. It'll be us, of course, and Nancy. She can bring someone with her if she chooses."

"Peggy will be there for Sharon."

"We'll spend our honeymoon night in a hotel and

then return home."

"You're unbelievable. I couldn't be happier."

"Let's eat up!"

We finished our meal and I cleaned up. A group message was sent relaying the same information and congratulations to me from my loving friends.

Nancy
Chapter Thirty

Judy and Carl arrived late yesterday afternoon. We ordered in pizza for supper, which eased my workload. My heart went out to Will and Bradley every time I thought of them. It was the closing or end of another chapter of my life.

For the funeral, I rode with Judy and Carl. It was so much fun to be with them. He doted on her and she loved it. It reminded me of being with Mike. At times like this, I felt so lonesome and missed him dearly, however, Will seemed to understand me. He was beginning to wiggle his way into my heart. It felt good.

When we arrived at the church, media cars filled the parking lot and up and down the street. We were lucky to find a spot within a short distance of walking and we met up with Peggy. The mortuary staff kept the media people at bay while we entered and found Will in the chapel.

Vicky and Diane were snuggled together in the casket and looked at peace. Tears filled my eyes as I silently said my goodbye to another close friend. Judy and I clung to each other, with Carl and Will beside us. Bradley stood off to the side and so did Peggy. Sharon had her ministerial robe on and held the Bible. It was a small ceremony for only close relatives and friends. Bradley didn't want a circus and neither did Will. Both wanted to get on with their lives.

Sharon spoke of the fun we had as children and growing up in such innocent times only to have a life sabotaged by a maniac. Bradley clamped his eyes shut, I noticed, and I reached for his hand to squeeze.

The ceremony was completed at the cemetery.

The seven of us went out to eat. The family hadn't requested a church luncheon because of the nature of the deaths. A restaurant near the Southdale Mall seated us.

After we received our drinks, Sharon made an announcement:

"Tomorrow at ten, we'll witness the marriage between Judy and Carl at Bethany. We won't have time to dawdle."

"Why not?" I said. "Something's up your sleeve."

"Well," Sharon said and looked up her sleeve. "Peggy and I have an appointment at City Hall with the Justice of the Peace at 11:30."

"Yay!" I said. Peggy beamed from cheek to cheek. "Peggy, you look like a ray of sunshine."

"I feel like one, too."

"Cheers!" we all said in unison.

Before we all said our good night, Will gave me a sweet kiss on the lips, which warmed me all over. My loneliness kept slipping away.

We drove home.

I popped in an old movie for us to watch, but Judy and Carl went to bed early. Eventually, I fell asleep on the couch. About midnight, I woke only to shut the TV off and go to bed.

We woke early and dressed. I wore a sparkly red dress and heels for such an occasion. Judy hadn't asked for me to be her matron of honor, but I figured she would. I drove separately, stopping to pick up two bouquets, for me and a fancier one for Judy plus a boutonnière for Carl and Will. I chose red and pink for the colors since it was close to the holidays.

Judy changed once they arrived at church. She looked magnificent in a long red velvet scooped neck dress and heels. Carl wore a suit. It wasn't long afterward that Will arrived, wearing his suit. Bradley had left for his apartment in Glenwood and back to work with plans to move into Will's house until he found his own place.

Judy looked at me and motioned for me to stand beside her. I presented her the bouquet. She pinned the flower on Carl and I did the same for Will. The ceremony began with Sharon as the officiate and Peggy sang, "How Great Thou Art," once it was over.

There was little time to spend congratulating the newlyweds because we had to go directly to City Hall in downtown. Will asked me to join him, which I did.

It took a while to maneuver through the streets of downtown and find a space on a nearby parking ramp. Once inside the building, we followed the newlyweds and the other two toward the judge's chamber where the ceremony was performed without much flourish.

Afterward, we gathered in the front hallway to discuss where to eat.

The two brides suggested the Thunderbird at the Mall of America.

I was happy to be Will's passenger. The last few days, weeks, had taken their toll on me. I was exhausted.

"Thanks for joining me," Will said.

"How has it been with Bradley?"

"Wonderful. His life was put on hold. He's pleasant. He cleaned up the dishes. He made his bed. He was so polite."

"That almost explains what kind of strict life he grew up with. He must've had an awful life to be so polite," I said.

"I don't know. I'm not a psychiatrist, but it's possible."

"At least now, he can breathe."

Will took me to my car and we made plans to meet over the weekend. He kissed me good night and I went on my way home.

Later, I received a group message instigated by Judy.

She said: *I'm wearing my secret purchase tonight.*

Sharon said: *Me too.*

I said: *I think it'll happen next weekend.*

We sent each other a heart.

The End

Sneak a look:

AN EXCERPT FROM Edith Wilson:

FOURTEEN POINTS TO DEATH

A WHITE HOUSE DOLLHOUSE SERIES

Chapter One

I woke early to a beautiful summer day.

Before leaving home, I kissed my handsome husband, Aaron, and walked out the door. The walk to my White House store near downtown Minneapolis, brought me past several ground-out cigarette butts near the bar appropriately named The Establishment. The rest of the way wound near the Mississippi River and a small park where children played, plus the old Grain Belt Brewery, now a library. There's also a bike trail. In a few short minutes, I was unlocking the store's back door.

I wanted to spend a few minutes with my assistant, Nancy. Nancy bears an uncanny resemblance to First Lady Edith Wilson. I'm not the only one who's noticed; when Russ Lippmann, a Woodrow Wilson biographer, director and owner of the neighborhood theater met Nancy, he immediately sought her for a role. His Rose Garden Theater featured historical plays about First Ladies and he thought Nancy would be perfect for their new play about Edith Wilson.

I promised to help Nancy learn her lines, as it

would give me a chance to find out more about Edith Wilson. I knew only a bit about her, and wanted to learn more.

The back door was still locked, so I knew that Max, my upstairs renter, wasn't up, and that Nancy hadn't arrived. The security code was Dolley Madison's birthdate. After punching it into the pad, I opened the door and stepped inside.

In the workroom, I found a doll's head carved, which meant that Max (who was also my employee), had spent the previous evening carving it. It's my job to paint the doll's head. Today I would paint Edith Wilson's face. My clients liked the natural look of my dolls. I sew the inaugural gowns, but not the Presidents' outfits. Those are easily purchased from a store in New Jersey. When the dolls are ready, then they're sold with the appropriate White House dollhouse. With my cell phone, I took a moment to send Max a message to tell him the head was beautiful. As I hit send, a new message popped on the screen from Nancy. She wanted to know if a blueberry muffin and coffee were on the agenda? Of course I said, yes!

I walked into the showroom, and took a minute to glance around. I made sure that the autographed pictures of First Ladies balanced evenly and that my framed doctoral diploma hung behind the computer where the checkout counter and cash register stood. Another wall featured my collection of miniature dollhouses and beside them my Penny dolls. I gave them a once-over with a duster, pinching my nose to avoid the particles.

Two days ago, I'd purchased Wilson memorabilia from a First Ladies descendant only online site. I'd purchased Edith Wilson's dollhouse and number of her papers plus a diary. I'm distantly related to Dolley Madison, and the site is privately owned by an Adams descendant. I wanted to show the dollhouse to Inga who owns the antique store on the opposite end of the block from the theater. I displayed it near the storefront window to draw in customers. My shop is just a short hop, skip, and a jump from the Mississippi River, which flows over St. Anthony Falls. The falls once harnessed energy to mill Gold Medal and Pillsbury flour. The other side of the river is downtown Minneapolis. This neighborhood is home to some of the oldest buildings in the city. Not far down Main Street is the historic Stone Arch Bridge, built by James J. Hill, the railroad magnate. I was pleased that our location fit right in with all the nearby historic sites.

I gazed out the front window. The cobblestone street slowed a few motorists, but not all. Russ Lippmann walked past, heading toward the theater. He glanced in my direction, changed his course, and entered my store.

"Russ, how nice of you to come in."

"I'm sorry I haven't taken the time to look around." Russ smiled as he gazed around the room. "My mother would love one of these houses."

"Who was her favorite First Lady?"

"Oh, probably Abigail Adams. She loved how

Abigail told John not to forget the ladies."

"Our first champion for equal rights," I said. "It's too bad that Abigail had such trouble with arthritis and couldn't travel much. She wasn't in the best of health once John became president."

"The historical White House is so plain compared to the one we have nowadays, isn't it?"

"Yes, and more gracious looking, I think."

"More welcoming—like come in and have a look around," Russ said. "I love it. Once the production run is finished, I'll bring Mother down here to take a look."

"Thank you. I'm looking forward to it."

Russ walked out the door. I watched him as he headed toward the theater and thought how his silhouette reminded me of the former president, Woodrow Wilson. I turned toward the sound of the back door opening.

More about Barbara Schlichting

Barbara Schlichting lives in northern, Minnesota, with her husband. She has two grown boys and five grandchildren. Since Minnesota is a hockey state, she cheers her grandchildren play on their respective teams as much as possible. Barbara is the author of the White House Dollhouse Mystery Series and a 1943 historical mystery. She also published poetry and two picture books.

You can write to Barbara Schlichting at

schlichtingbarb@gmail.com.

You may also contact her through her website.

www.barbaraschlichting.com. If you so choose, you may sign up for the newsletter on the website.

BOOK CLUB QUESTIONS.

1. What part of your life mirrors Nancy's? When? What age?
2. Do you think Nancy regrets her early engagement to Mike? If so, why?
3. How did Nancy feel when she learned about the sale of Mike's house and why?
4. Why was it so hard for Sharon to tell Nancy about Mike's life and death?
5. What effect did Margo's death have on Nancy? Judy? Sharon?
6. Why do you think Judy chose to live in Madison, WI, and not MN?
7. What thoughts went through your mind when Bradley was located?
8. Why did Bradley kill his father?
9. Did the story ending give you peace?
10. What people in your life do you wonder about? Why?

CPSIA information can be obtained
at www.ICGtesting.com
Printed in the USA
FFHW021716210619
53139483-58793FF